A few unruly curls had escaped the wide band meant to keep them in place and were now stuck to her moist cheeks.

Cody's fingers itched to be able to lift them away and tuck them behind her ears. But he didn't dare. He already loved this job, and he wasn't going to spoil anything by getting offside with this particular doctor.

So why was he wrapping his arms around her and hauling her shaking body close to his? Because he needed to hold her against him. However briefly, whatever the outcome, he just *did*. Tucking her head against his chest, he dropped his chin on top of her thick, soft hair and held her. Breathed in her scent of citrus and residual fear. In his arms she gave him strength, helped him settle his jittery muscles. He hoped he was giving the same back.

She's a perfect fit for my body.

The realisation banged through him, made him tense. Made Harper lift her head and look at him with puzzlement beaming out at him from watery eyes.

She sniffed once, and plastered a tight smile on her mouth. 'Let's go face the second round. There'll be questions from all directions.'

Slowly Cody unwound his arms from that warm body he shouldn't be noticing in any way. From somewhere deep he found a smile that was entirely for her. 'You did good, Doctor. Really good.'

Dear Reader,

I'm often asked where the ideas for my stories come from, so I thought I'd share the wee nudge I got for this story.

At the Romance Writers of New Zealand conference there was a young guy working at the bar in the lounge, serving everything from coffees to cocktails and a multitude of drinks in between. He charmed everyone with his enthusiasm and willingness to keep his customers more than happy.

Louisa George and I commented that he'd make a great hero for a story. His name was Cody—and that, plus the little I've already mentioned, was the start of my hero in this story.

My Cody started his working life as a deep-sea fisherman, but eventually followed his heart into nursing. A strong man like that needs a strong woman, and along comes Harper—a doctor with a soft heart, especially around children, which makes it downright tragic that she can't have her own.

I hope you enjoy following these two through their highs and lows as they try to stay true to their needs.

I'd love to hear from you at sue.mackay56@yahoo.com, or visit my website at suemackay.co.nz.

Cheers!

Sue

DR WHITE'S
BABY WISH

BY
SUE MacKAY

Published in Great Britain 2016
By Mills & Boon, an imprint of HarperCollins*Publishers*
1 London Bridge Street, London, SE1 9GF

© 2016 Sue MacKay

ISBN: 978-0-263-06516-9

Our policy is to use papers that are natural, renewable and recyclable
products and made from wood grown in sustainable forests. The logging
and manufacturing processes conform to the legal environmental
regulations of the country of origin.

Printed and bound in Great Britain
by CPI Antony Rowe, Chippenham, Wiltshire

Sue MacKay lives with her husband in New Zealand's beautiful Marlborough Sounds, with the water at her doorstep and birds and trees at the back door. It is the perfect setting to indulge her passions of entertaining friends by cooking them sumptuous meals, drinking fabulous wine, going for hill walks or kayaking around the bay—and, of course, writing stories.

Books by Sue MacKay

Mills & Boon Medical Romance

Doctors to Daddies
A Father for Her Baby
The Midwife's Son

The Gift of a Child
From Duty to Daddy
A Family This Christmas
The Family She Needs
Midwife...to Mum!
Reunited...in Paris!
A December to Remember
Breaking All Their Rules

Visit the Author Profile page
at millsandboon.co.uk for more titles.

CHAPTER ONE

'RESUSCITATED CARDIAC ARREST coming in from Court-
ney Place,' the newest nurse in Wellington Central Hospital's emergency department called as he banged the
wall phone back on its hook. 'Male, fifty-two, revived
by bystander using CPR. ETA less than five minutes.'

'Thanks, Cody,' Dr Harper White replied. 'Resus
Two when he gets here.'

Cody Brand added quietly so that only she heard,
'Apparently intoxicated as well.' The man was shaking
his head. 'Seems a bit early in the day.'

Harper's gaze flicked to the wall clock. Eleven forty-
five. Early? Hardly. Not in the world of accidents and
incidents. 'Hopefully now a very subdued man.'

'You think he's thanking his lucky stars and swearing off the booze for good?' Cody grinned. 'Good luck
with that.'

That grin could get the man anything—though not
from her. But she'd have to concentrate on not giving
in to the zingy feeling skimming her skin. 'I guess it is
wishful thinking.' Harper watched as Cody strode into
Resus Two and began checking equipment, despite it
having been restocked and double-checked less than an
hour ago after a middle-aged patient had been treated

for a major allergic reaction to something she'd eaten for breakfast.

The new nurse left nothing to chance—something Harper appreciated but which also annoyed her at times. Other staff in the department did their jobs just as well. She gave a mental shrug. Maybe Nurse Brand was still settling in and she should leave him to it. No one else had complained, and it was far better than him being slack.

Turning away, she rubbed her temples with her fingertips, trying to relieve the tension building behind her eyes. She did not need a migraine. She had a fun weekend to look forward to, with a birthday party not to be missed. Reaching for the next patient file on the stack, she determined not to let a migraine or the nurse's well-muscled thighs and wide shoulders that blue scrubs did little to hide distract her.

'Why pick up a file when any moment now the ambulance's due to deliver? It's not like you've got time to treat someone else.' Karin, a registrar, grinned. 'Hottie's got to you, hasn't he?'

'I don't think so.' She hurriedly dropped the file back in place.

'You're made of stone?'

Harper tried not to smile but it was impossible not to. 'The man's built, no doubt about it.'

'I'd be worried if you hadn't noticed.' Karin picked up the file Harper had discarded.

'Like I'm looking for another man.' Harper glanced at her sidekick, who was also staring after Cody.

'Maybe not looking *for*, but you were definitely looking *at*.'

Yeah, she had been. 'You're single, so what's holding you back?' Harper retorted.

'Not my type. But you, on the other hand, need to get back in the saddle and—'

'Don't go there,' Harper interrupted, grateful for the shrill ring of the emergency phone yet again. For once the busy morning made her happy, if only because it would shut Karin up. No doubt only briefly, as the woman was known to talk far too much about things she should keep her mouth closed on.

Nurse Brand had picked up the phone instantly, and Harper couldn't help but take another appreciative glance. He'd been here five days and labelled 'Hottie' by the female staff within hours of starting. She couldn't argue with the name. No one could. He was made to be looked at—drooled over, even—but that was where it stopped as far as she was concerned.

For one, she worked with him, and this was her dream job, working with a dedicated group of highly skilled people all focused on helping their patients coping with difficult and often tragic situations. So far, what she'd seen of the latest nurse to join them had impressed her. He fitted right in. He might be easy going with those he worked with, but the moment someone suffering in any way at all came near him they had his undivided attention as he took care of them.

And, if she needed another reason to not be interested in him, it was that she'd had all the disappointment from men she ever needed. The ink was barely dry on the divorce papers from her last blunder.

Aren't you getting ahead of yourself? The guy treats you the same as every other person in the department with his charming disposition, his easy smile and relaxed wit. Why would you be special?

The phone was slammed back into its cradle. 'Suspected body packer coming in from the international airport,' Cody informed her. That deep, husky voice that reminded her of things she had no right to be thinking of sounded calm and focused on work, putting her in her place without even trying. 'Twenty-three-year-old male collapsed during an interview with Customs officers after nervous behaviour when a sniffer dog indicated on him.'

Harper groaned inwardly. She hated these cases. If the guy was carrying internally and had collapsed it suggested a balloon containing heroin or cocaine had burst. She'd lost a young female mule last year, and had seen another die years back when she'd been specialising in Auckland. It was a fast but very painful way to die. But she was getting ahead of herself. It was only supposition that the man was a mule, that a package had burst and that he'd die as a result. 'ETA?'

'Ten. Resus One?' Cody asked.

'Yes. I want you with me on this. Karin, you take the cardiac victim.'

'No problem,' Karin answered with a chuckle.

Harper scowled. She had not demanded Cody work with her because of his sex appeal. 'I need someone strong nearby in case the patient tries to fight us as we work on him. If he's absorbing cocaine or heroin he'll become aggressive as the pain gets worse.' No one else in the department came as big and, she presumed, as strong as Nurse Brand. 'I'm hoping the guy's suffering from dehydration after a long flight, or even the flu, but until I know for certain we have to be prepared for anything.'

Karin leaned close and said, so only Harper could hear, 'Hottie would make nice babies.'

'Shut it,' she hissed, now getting more than mildly annoyed. She couldn't have babies with any man no matter how hot he might be. It just wasn't possible when she didn't have a womb.

The bell rang, indicating a patient had arrived by ambulance. Unfortunately too soon to be hers, Harper thought. She needed a diversion about now. Karin didn't know how her comment hurt. It wasn't something she talked about, even when it should be old hat. Especially after what had happened with Darren. *Suck it up,* she growled at herself and followed Cody into Resus One.

Cody was already getting a fan out of the cupboard.

'You've dealt with a case like this before?' she asked him.

He shook his head. 'No, but I've read up on it. Soaring temps which have to be brought down fast if we want to save him, right?'

'Yes. Apart from that and the agitation, he'll also have high BP and could be fitting. *If* he's carrying and has absorbed a drug, which we don't know for sure yet,' she repeated aloud. Crossing her fingers wasn't very medical, but sometimes anything and everything helped.

'Do we soak him in cold water if he has a temperature?'

She nodded. 'Grab some bottles from the staff fridge.' While Cody did that she went to check the drug cabinet for something to help calm the patient and slow any seizures he might have. If... This was still all about *if* the guy had swallowed packages of drugs in the first place. Why anyone would do that was beyond her. In her book no amount of money was worth risking her life for.

Minutes later the shrill ring of the bell from the ambulance bay sliced through Harper's thoughts and had her moving fast. There'd be no time to waste if this was the worst-case scenario. No surprise that as she raced towards the bay she found Cody striding right alongside her. He never missed a cue. She called over her shoulder to the nurses waiting at the desk, 'Matilda, Jess— Resus One, now.'

A paramedic joined them as his off-sider began rolling the stretcher into the department. 'Mick Frew. Very agitated, making it difficult to get any obs.'

'What readings have you got?' Cody asked even before Harper had opened her mouth.

'BP one-seventy over eighty-nine and rising. He's been fitting for the last five minutes. It's been tricky enough to keep the face mask on him, let alone do much else for him. I couldn't take his temp but by the feel of him he's burning up.'

Harper studied their patient as they rushed him through to Resus One where the other nurses waited, ready to take obs and put an oxygen mask on. This was sounding and looking more like a package had burst internally. Definitely more than a dose of flu or dehydration, but she had to be one-hundred percent sure before she committed to treating him. Something else could be causing these symptoms. 'How certain were the Customs officers that he'd taken drugs? Do you know?' she asked the paramedic.

'Of course he has' was the cutting retort from behind her.

Harper spun around and came face-to-face with a dapper man who had the coldest eyes she'd encountered in a long time. 'Who are you?' Ambulance crews wore uniforms, not expensive, perfectly pressed suits worn by the man stepping towards her from the direction of the ambulance bay.

He shrugged. 'He's carrying. Cocaine. In balloons.'

Just one of those bursting would mean trouble, serious trouble, for Mick Frew. What if more than one had come apart? 'You seem very sure. I repeat, who are you?'

His eyes were glacial. 'Detective Strong to you.' He walked beside the stretcher, his eyes flicking between the young man and her.

He wasn't acting like any detective she'd dealt with. Not even the one she'd been married to. 'Well, Detective, I need to know how sure you are.'

'He's packing.'

'Right.' She'd still check Frew thoroughly but it was looking more and more likely that he had ingested drugs. 'Thank you for your help. Now, you'll have to leave. You know the rules. Only hospital staff and patients are allowed into Resus.'

The detective grunted, and she thought he said, 'We'll see about that,' but right then her patient began kicking and waving his arms in the air, the pain obviously becoming unbearable.

Cody caught an arm inches from slamming into Harper's stomach. 'Easy, Mick. We're all here to help you. We need to get you onto the bed, okay?'

She nodded thanks at Cody. That fist would've hurt if it'd reached her.

The transfer was fast and awkward as everyone tried to hold those flailing limbs without dropping their patient. The paramedic handed over the Patient Report Form and was gone with his stretcher, no doubt glad to have got shot of his aggressive pick-up.

'Check for a medic-alert disc on his arm,' Harper instructed Cody. She was running out of other options but could not afford to overlook anything, including an existing medical condition. Truth? She didn't want this young guy dealing with what was becoming apparent to all of them.

'Nothing,' Cody noted as he took a hit on his upper arm. 'Mick, steady, man. You're in hospital. We're the good guys.'

Harper leaned as close as she dared, one eye on those flailing arms. 'Mick, I'm Harper, a doctor, and I want to help you, but I need to know if you've swallowed any drugs.'

The young guy groaned, opening and closing his eyes rapidly.

'Yes or no?' she persisted.

A brief nod was his only reply.

'Balloons or capsules?'

Mick twisted his head to the side and stared briefly beyond her, fear and hatred blinking out of his stricken eyes. 'Balloons,' he croaked.

So the detective was right. The detective. She looked up, right into Cody's eyes, and saw her own uncertainty there which gave her the determination to get rid of the stranger. Turning around, she growled, 'I asked you to leave, Detective Strong.'

'So you did.' He sounded so smug a trickle of apprehension ran down her spine.

Cody said in a 'don't fool with me' tone, 'You will do as Dr White says.'

Nice as it was to have the nurse backing her, Harper had a definite feeling their visitor wasn't going to take any more notice of Cody than he had her. She glanced at Cody and nodded thanks again, appreciative of his attempt to help her with this horrid man. She didn't know why she thought him horrid, but she did. Probably something to do with those arctic-blue eyes that bored into her relentlessly. The complete opposite to the warmth she found in Cody's brief green gaze on the rare occasion he looked at her for an answer to some question.

Shivering, she glanced at the nurse now, not wanting to focus on that other man. But she still had to get rid of him. He was a hazard in the emergency room.

'Call security,' she mouthed at Cody.

Mick wheezed out some words.

'What did you say?' Leaning down to hear him better, Harper felt the heat radiating off his body. 'Jess, get the fan going as fast as possible.'

'Not cop. Supplier.'

'Mick? Really?'

He nodded. At least, that was what she thought his erratic head movement was.

Harper hoped against hope the man behind her hadn't heard or seen any of that. He wouldn't be pleased that she now knew for sure he wasn't a detective but a criminal. She thought fast. What to do? They had to work on saving Mick's life, get the so-called detective out of here and call in the real police, all at the same time. And she'd sent Cody out of the room. Squeezing the young man's hand, she whispered, 'Okay,' before straightening up.

Of course it was not okay. It was a minefield.

Cody was still there. Thank goodness. His presence and calm manner gave her strength. Catching her eye, he nodded once, tightly. Had he heard what their patient had said? Whatever message he was trying to send her, she wasn't understanding, and they were wasting time if Mick stood any chance at all of surviving the poison streaming through his body.

With a shaky breath she turned to the man causing her problems. 'This is an emergency department. Anything you want to ask my patient will have to wait until we've treated him.' *If he survives*. 'So please head out to the waiting area. Now.'

'Or what?' A rapid movement and a gun appeared between them.

'What are you doing?' she gasped as that trickle of apprehension became a torrent of fear. She was unable to stop staring at the weapon pointed directly at her chest, where her heart was beating the weirdest, sickest rhythm against her ribs. Definitely not a detective, then. Glancing out of the wide opening of Resus One, she could see only one person at the desk, and he was rapidly removing himself from sight. 'Call the police,' Harper begged silently.

'Hey, what do you think you're doing?' Cody moved around the bed fast, stepped up close to her so his arm touched hers and eyeballed her aggressor, anger darkening his face. 'Put that away.'

'You want to argue?' The man smirked as he waved the gun at Cody, taunting him to take a crack at him. 'I'm here to collect what's mine.'

That gun mesmerised Harper as it was moved between her and Cody in a very deliberate, menacing way. One little squeeze and someone could die. Just as simple, and horrific, as that.

She had to do something. Drawing what she hoped was a calming breath, but felt like an asthma attack, she said in a voice that didn't sound like hers, 'Stop this. Now. Our first priority's to save Mick's life. So get out of the way while we do all we can.' She glanced sideways to her patient. Damn. 'Cody, oxygen. Now. Jess, bring the fan closer. We need to get his temperature down fast.'

The girl was paralysed with fear. 'Sorry, yes, Harper.'

With Mick fighting him all the way, Cody struggled getting the mask on.

'Matilda, the water.' No reply. 'Matilda?' Harper glanced around but there was no sign of the junior nurse.

When had she snuck away? Now they were down to three. Not enough to help their patient, but fewer to be confronted with that gun. Hopefully it also meant they could expect help in the form of security or, better yet, armed police, shortly. Then what would *Detective* Strong do? Her skin lifted in goose bumps as she struggled to tamp down the fear threatening to rage through her and flatten her thought processes. Would they find themselves in the middle of a shooting match? She had a patient to care for; other staff to try and keep safe.

'The oxygen's flowing.' Cody's calm voice cut through her panic.

Her eyes met his and the fear backed off a few notches. Darn, but he was good. Cool as. She straightened her shoulders and dipped her chin to acknowledge she was on her game, however shakily.

Cody nodded back. 'I'll get the water.' He caught Mick's flying arm and tucked it down against the young man's body. 'Steady, mate. Think we'll strap you down for a bit, okay? Can't have you knocking out your doctor, can we? Jess, maybe you should get the water.'

Harper took the end of a strap he handed her. He had it all together—seemed completely unfazed about their unwanted spectator. She drew more strength from him. 'You and Jess do this while I go get some drugs.' She turned to come face-to-face with their interloper, and felt the cold, hard reality of a gun barrel poked into her stomach.

'I don't think so.' Those chilly eyes fixed on her. 'No one's going anywhere.'

'I am trying to save this man's life—a life that you mightn't care about—' she stabbed his chest without thinking '—but I do. *We* do. So get out of my way.'

'The only thing I care about are those packs in his

gut. They belong to me.' Cold steel jabbed deep into her stomach. 'Nothing, no one else, matters. Get it?'

She nodded. 'Sure. But I am going to do my absolute best to save Mick's life, whatever you think, so move out of my way.' She locked eyes with the man, fighting down the returning panic weaving through her tense muscles.

He waved the gun in her face, so close she tipped her head back. 'What are you going to do about it, doc? Eh? Wait until idiot here dies? Because he's going to. One way or the other. They all do.'

The firearm was menacing but even more so were the eyes locked on her as he continued. 'Save us all the trouble and cut him open so I get what I came for. Then I'll get out of your hair.' If he'd shouted or snarled, she'd have handled his statement better, but he'd spoken softly, clearly, and set her quivering with dread.

There was no getting rid of the man, nor was he going to let her get the midazolam Mick desperately needed. She wanted to call out for someone else to bring the drug but that meant putting another person in jeopardy.

'I'll go,' Cody intervened. He flicked her a quick look that seemed to say, *Hang in there, I'm on to this,* but she could be far off the mark. It had been a very fast glance.

The gunman snarled, 'No you don't.'

Cody shrugged exaggeratedly. 'We need more water and drugs and, if you think I'd do a bunk and leave Dr White alone with you, think again. The drugs cupboard is just on the other side of the doorway.'

Phew. Relief warmed Harper. As much as she'd like the nurse out of here and safe, she didn't want to be left without him watching her back as much as it was possible.

Her relief lasted nanoseconds. An arm slung around

her throat, cutting off anything she could've said to back up Cody. Her assailant hauled her backwards, hard up against his torso.

'Let her go.' Cody stood right in front of them, his hands loose at his sides, those impressive feet spread wide, looking for all the world like he regularly dealt with this sort of situation, this type of villain.

'Want to try and make me?' the man snarled, then tightened his hold around Harper's neck. Was he getting upset that things weren't quite going his way?

They weren't going her way either, but she could try to regain some control over the situation. Struggling to straighten up, she got hauled further off-balance for her efforts.

The grip tightened on Harper's throat, making her eyes water and feel as though they could pop out of their sockets any moment. Her windpipe hurt. But it was the latest wave of fear rolling up from her stomach that really threw her off-centre. She didn't have a chance of getting away from this man, or of saving Mick.

Mick. 'Let me go,' she tried to say, but nothing got past that arm pushing on her throat. Her fingers clawed at it, trying to loosen the throttling sensation. She couldn't swallow and breathing was a strain.

Her eyes fixed on Cody's. She hoped he couldn't see her fear. Looking deep into his steady gaze, she tried to draw strength from him, to calm down. She couldn't afford to let the assailant beat her. *Count to ten, think what to do.*

How in Hades did she count when even getting enough oxygen into her lungs was a mission?

Cody gulped. Strong was hurting Harper. But she was good. She might be terrified—he definitely was—but she wasn't taking any crap from the lowlife. *Go, girl.* No. *Be careful, stay safe.* Lowlife had the advantage and not once had he looked as though he'd be afraid to pull that trigger.

He guessed the guy had nothing to lose. No one would stop him walking out of here while he held that gun. Hopefully the armed-defenders unit would arrive soon and be able to work out a solution without anyone getting injured or worse. If someone in the department had dialled 111. If Matilda had stopped to tell anyone on her mad dash to freedom. He was afraid to look out into the department in case he alerted Lowlife to other staff or anyone that might be working towards taking him down.

In the meantime the three of them still stuck in here had to deal with the situation and keep out of harm's way. They weren't going to get the drug that might calm Mick down a little. The odds were stacking up against him as time ran out fast. And, while Cody abhorred drugs and the people who made a living out of them, this young man was paying a huge price, way too huge. He wouldn't be making the big bucks that people like Lowlife here would be. 'I'll run towels under the cold tap,' he told Harper. 'Then you outline what we do next.' He was trying to warn her to stay put, that they'd get this sorted.

But either she was playing dumb or was just being plain brave because she shook her head, and managed to speak, which indicated that the arm had loosened on her throat. 'We need icy-cold water, not tap water.'

Lowlife tightened his grip around Harper's neck again and heavily tapped the gun barrel against her skull. 'No one goes anywhere or the doc gets it.'

Harper's eyes widened and all the colour drained

from her cheeks. Her front teeth dug deep into her bottom lip.

'Let her go,' Cody growled. Fury was building inside him. 'Incapacitating her isn't going to change a thing.' It was obviously a painful hold. Her throat was going to hurt for days. He gritted his teeth. It was crazy to think anyone would have to deal with an assailant in a place where people came to get fixed up, but it happened.

Another man threatening a woman on his watch, though? No, it wasn't happening again.

'You think I won't use this? Huh? Want to see what happens when a bullet goes through brain matter?' Lowlife laughed, a hideous sound that must've been heard throughout the department and made Cody's skin crawl.

But it was the shock in Harper's eyes that really got to him. She probably hadn't encountered anything quite like this before, while he had. He had held his wife in his arms while she'd died of a knife wound to her heart. He'd been unable to halt the life draining out of her that day—had felt so useless, so helpless. Which was why the quiet evil about this man tightened his gut and had him fearing for Harper. That fear vied with anger. Nothing he said or did helped Harper while she was trying to help her patient. She did not deserve to be held to ransom. Or worse. Evil had no boundaries.

All the things he hated about bullies and nasty SOBs burst through him, and it took every ounce of self-control not to leap on the guy and take him down. That would really help the situation. Not. He'd probably get Harper killed in the process. He would not face that again. Once in a lifetime was once too often. He had to be careful; acting impulsively only led to disaster. 'Let's be sensible here. Dr White cannot save Mick's life while you're holding her.' Damn, but he hated grovelling.

'Who says we need to save the useless piece of garbage? I only want my drugs out.'

Jeez. Cody rammed his fingers through his hair. This guy didn't deserve to be breathing. 'Still need the doctor for that.' Though Lowlife probably had his own knife strapped somewhere on his body; Cody had no illusions about the man getting his merchandise back himself. Which only underlined the dire situation they were all in.

Harper blinked at him. Mouthed something he couldn't read. Her eyes tracked sideways towards the head of the bed.

The monitor? Reluctant to take his eyes off Lowlife while he held that gun to Harper, Cody quickly glanced sideways and saw the flat line on the screen. Mick Frew had gone into cardiac arrest. He hadn't even heard the changed electronic sound; he'd been so focused on the doctor and her captor.

Cody needed to act quickly before anyone else rushed in to help and found themselves in this dangerous situation. He immediately hit in the centre of Mick's sternum with his clenched hand, watching the screen intently. The flat line continued. Another thump and he said as calmly as possible, 'Paddles, Jess.' It wasn't Mick's condition churning his gut, but Harper's. Dealing with this cardiac arrest wasn't going to quieten Lowlife any, but no way could he ignore their patient either.

Thankfully Jess already had the paddles in her hands, even if she was staring at Harper.

As he shoved the paddles firmly onto Mick's exposed chest, he couldn't stop thinking about the doctor behind him. She was amazing, more concerned about their patient than her own life. She'd read the monitor, or heard it go into that monotone that went with lack of heartbeats, and had tried to let him know even when her windpipe was being squashed. She was some lady. *Careful, pal. Don't get too impressed. You'd hate to follow that up with something more caring.*

He held the paddles in place and said urgently, forcefully, 'Stand back.'

'Want to get closer, doc?' Lowlife chuckled.

Cody froze. Never before had he heard such an evil chuckle. It was a match for that hideous laugh. He tried for reasoned and calm. Tried very hard. Snarled, 'Stand back. If the doctor gets zapped, so will you.' Dumb idiot. Hadn't thought of that, had he?

Behind him Harper was hauled back so fast she lost her balance and fell into the man behind her, who also lost his balance.

The hand holding the gun wavered, the fingers tightening as Lowlife struggled to remain upright.

The air stuck in Cody's chest as he waited for the explosion as the trigger was inadvertently pulled. It didn't happen.

Instead, Harper dropped lower, fell to the floor. Deliberately? Lowlife no longer had her by the throat, or the gun at her head. Cody sprang forward, his shoulder aimed directly for the assailant's chest. They went down together, sprawling across the floor while the gun spun out of reach.

Harper crawled after the weapon as Cody worked at subduing Strong by flipping him on to his stomach and planting a knee in the small of his back. 'Don't even bother trying to get away.' Sometimes it was a bonus being a big man, Cody admitted as he looked around for Harper.

She was standing now, holding the gun as though it

was about to go off and shoot her. Her hands were shaking and her eyes were wide with shock.

Cody's heart squeezed for her.

Jess called from the bed in a terrified voice, 'Still no sign of cardiac function.'

Harper blinked, shook her head abruptly and shoved the gun into the waistband of her scrubs. Rushing across to pick up the paddles from where Cody had dropped them moments ago, she instructed, 'Stand back,' and delivered a jolt of electricity. And another, and another.

'Jess,' Cody called as the man under his knee squirmed and started swearing loudly. 'Go get help. Let everyone know we've got Strong under control, but as soon as the police arrive I'm more than happy to hand him over.'

Harper was zapping Mick like her life depended on it. 'Come on. Don't leave us now.' Tears ran down her cheeks and her bottom lip trembled.

'Harper. Stop.' Cody desperately wanted to go and wrap his arms around her, take away some of the shock presumably making her react like that. As if he'd get away with doing that. Even in the circumstances he knew Dr Harper White would not thank him for showing her concern—especially in front of the staff. Her reputation for being strong, solid and independent went before her, and in the week he'd been working here he hadn't seen anything to negate it.

Suddenly the room was full of gun-toting men dressed in the dark-blue overalls of the armed defenders squad and Cody relaxed for the first time in what seemed like hours but according to the wall clock was little more than ten minutes.

He couldn't help himself prodding the man beneath him as he stood up. 'You're history.' What he really wanted to do to the guy wasn't going to happen even though the creep deserved every moment of pain for what he'd done to Harper White. The fear in her eyes would stay with him for a long time. And then the anger. She was something else; she really was.

As cops grabbed their man, Cody crossed to Harper. 'It's over, doctor.'

Her hands were shaking as he took the paddles from her. 'Mick—he didn't stand a chance.'

As her fingers oh-so-gently closed Mick's eyes she said quietly, 'I'm sorry, Mick Frew. I am so sorry.' Then she slashed her sleeve across her face. 'Damn.'

Cody muttered around the road block in his throat, 'We weren't exactly given much of a chance.'

Watery eyes met his as her fingers went to her temples, rubbed hard. 'Unfortunately you're right.' Then she straightened up to her full height, bringing her head to somewhere about his shoulder.

A few unruly curls had escaped the wide band meant to keep them in place and were now stuck to her moist cheeks. Cody's fingers itched to be able to lift them away and tuck them behind her ears. But he didn't dare. He already loved this job, and wasn't going to spoil anything by getting offside with this particular doctor.

So why was he wrapping his arms around her and hauling her shaking body close to his? Because he needed to hold her against him. However briefly, whatever the outcome, he just did. Tucking her head against his chest, he dropped his chin on the top of her thick, soft hair and held her. Breathed in her scent of citrus and residual fear. Her being in his arms gave him strength, helped him settle his jittery muscles. He hoped he was giving the same back.

She's a perfect fit for my body. The realisation banged through him, made him tense.

Made Harper lift her head and look at him with puzzlement beaming out at him from watery eyes. She sniffed once and plastered a tight smile on her mouth. 'Let's go face the second round. There'll be questions from all directions.'

Slowly Cody unwound his arms from that warm body he shouldn't be noticing in any way. From somewhere deep he found a smile that was entirely for her. 'You did good, doctor. Really good.'

CHAPTER TWO

REALLY? I DID a good job? Of what? Harper asked herself as she stepped out of Resus One. Their patient was dead, the assailant had been taken down by Cody and she felt like a toddler who'd just had a huge sugar fix. The shaking had started in earnest now that she had nothing to focus on. That impending migraine had also become reality.

Turning to Cody, she saw his jaw tighten. His mouth flat-lined. Feeling out of sorts too? He'd been so calm in there, so reliable. Yet she'd felt a tremor in his body in that all too brief moment he'd held her close. His hug had been like a welcoming home, a comfort, a much-needed place of calm and care and warmth. Only during that hug had she known for sure how rattled he'd been by what had gone down. She liked that he'd shared the whole episode, including the fear. She stepped closer to him, still needing his strength, his deliberate calm.

Which was enough to make her step away again. She must not need anything about him, from him. Needing something from a man had got her into trouble before, had led to the wrong marriage for her.

'Hey, Harper, are you all right?' George stepped up to her. He was head of the department and her brother's friend—which meant Jason would already know about this, damn it all.

She swallowed, pain from where her throat had been flattened more apparent now she wasn't on high alert. 'I'm fine.' Her voice came out as a high-pitched squeak. Great. Now she was sounding like that sugar-overloaded toddler.

The department was in chaos with police going about their business while nurses and doctors hovered around the area, looking like they didn't know what to do or where to go, so they resorted to staring at Cody and her.

George took her arm. 'My office. Both of you. Jess, you too. Where's Matilda?'

Jess shook her head. 'I don't know. I haven't seen her. I'm on lunch break now, so can I go to the canteen? My boyfriend's there.'

'Of course you can, as soon as you've talked to the police. They'll want to ask you all a few things.' George looked around at his staff. 'Okay, everyone, we have a waiting room full of patients, and one in the ambulance bay. Let's try to get back to normal as quickly and quietly as possible. The police will be here for a while, and I expect you to be helpful and answer any of their questions.' He held a hand up. 'However, I do not want any one telling patients what has happened.'

Harper grimaced. Like he had any hope of every single person in the department keeping their mouth shut, but she supposed he had to put it out there. Texts would already be flying around the city, probably the whole country, and the moment Jess saw her boyfriend she'd be yabbering her head off. Not that Harper could blame the girl. Talking was a way of relieving the stress. Even she felt a desire to tell someone what had happened, but she wouldn't. That would be totally unlike her. But then how often did she have a gun held to her head? Her muscles tightened as renewed fear grabbed her.

'Cody, Harper, come with me. I'll get you coffee sent from the cafeteria shortly. And some food.' George's answer to everything was coffee followed by food. 'Come on. The sooner you talk to the police, the sooner I can send you home for the day.'

Harper shook her head. 'You said the waiting room's full. I can't just disappear.' At least, that was what she tried to say, but her voice was raspy and all broken up. Now that she was no longer dealing with the assailant and everything else, the pain in her throat seemed to be taking over. She needed something else to concentrate on so it would go on the back burner, at least until she got home.

Beside her, Cody growled, 'I'm sure the other doctors don't expect you back on the floor today.' Then his hands clenched at his sides. 'Gawd, what I don't want to do to that lowlife.'

'Not happening,' she croaked.

'Look what he's done to you, all because of his greed.'

It hadn't been only her. She spoke slowly and tried to ignore the pain. 'George, Jess is in shock. Someone needs to check her over.'

'On to it.'

She placed a hand on Cody's forearm. Since when had she done this 'touching colleagues' stuff? She guessed that gun had a lot to answer for. Working hard at getting her words out clearly, she said, 'Don't let him get to you. I'm all right. Truly.'

Cody covered her hand with his for a quick touch, sending his warmth through her. Again. She could get used to that. But she wouldn't.

'You're more than all right,' he muttered before glaring across the room to where the assailant was being hauled roughly out of the department by two cops.

He no longer looked quite so dapper or smug, but the eyes that locked on her momentarily were filled with hatred.

She shivered. 'Evil. Pure evil.' As Harper watched the man being taken away, she felt some relief seep into her body and loosen a little of the tension gripping her. Turning to Cody, she asked, 'How are you feeling?' She swallowed and kept going. 'You were right in the middle of it all. You hit the floor hard when you leapt on him.' She still couldn't get the sight of him doing that out of her head, probably wouldn't for days.

Eyes the colour of spring paddocks locked on her. 'Think my hip took a bit of a hammering but I didn't feel a thing at the time. I'll probably know about it tomorrow.' His wide mouth tipped upward into a beautiful smile that sent ripples of pleasure through her. He really was ridiculously good-looking.

'Ouch.' She didn't know if she was referring to his hip or her reaction to him.

His smile, like that hug, enveloped her in the sensation that they were in this together and that no one else had a part in it. Sort of like being in a cocoon with just Cody, which gave her a sense of it not being all bad. Not that she could find anything good about the last twenty or so minutes. She'd lost a patient. She hated that. No matter that the odds had been stacked against Mick from the moment he'd swallowed those drugs; she'd have done everything possible to turn the situation around—*if* she'd been given half a chance. *If* seemed to be the word of the day.

Someone tapped Harper's shoulder, and she nearly

jumped out of her skin. Spinning around, she half-expected to find the gunman standing there smirking at her. 'Don't touch— Oh. Sorry, George.' She'd totally overreacted. She rubbed her temples to calm herself down and try to ease the pounding that had cranked up harder than ever.

George gave her an understanding look. 'Take it easy. He's gone, Harper.'

'Yes.' He had, but how long before the sense of dread he'd caused left her? Going to sleep tonight might be a lot more difficult than usual.

'The police want statements from all four of you. Especially you and Cody. That's not happening in here with patients being treated. They'd overhear everything.' Despite the presence of the armed defenders and two detectives, the department head was in charge, and letting her know it even before she argued that she needed to be busy right now.

If—that damned word again—she was being honest, she knew she wasn't in any fit state to be dealing with emergencies or even the mundane illnesses presenting at the moment. But the idea of sitting in the office doing nothing but answering endless questions made her sick to the stomach. Glancing at Cody, she saw sympathy in his gaze. *I don't need sympathy. Especially not from you when you probably feel much the same way I do.* She had to admit he didn't look at all fazed by any of this, but he had been shaky in that hug. 'I suppose coffee would be good,' she conceded.

'I'm surprised you think you can swallow anything.' Cody watched Harper struggling to cope with the aftermath of the assault. She looked annoyed and a tad bewildered. No longer fearful, though, thank goodness.

What would she do if he hugged her again? She held her hands against her stomach with her fingers entwined and knuckles white. He suspected she was desperately hanging on to her self-control. The shock was catching up, and he wasn't immune either.

'I'll manage,' she snapped. Was getting feisty another way of covering up her feelings?

'Shouldn't one of our doctors take a look at your throat?' he asked. There could've been serious damage done.

'That's next on my agenda. You really shouldn't talk too much until everything's settled down.' George nodded at Harper. 'Want me to talk to Jason as well?'

'No.' Harper shook her head sharply at the boss, her eyes glittering angrily. 'No.' Then, 'I presumed you already had.'

'Been a bit busy. You do realise someone will have put it out there on the net? Jason probably already knows, and the rest of your family.' George gave her a pointed look.

If that throat had been in proper working order Cody had no doubt she'd have been telling George where to go, and it wouldn't be somewhere nice. She wasn't known for holding back on her thoughts, no matter who she was talking to. Who was Jason anyway? Her partner? She didn't wear a wedding ring. He had to be a significant person in her life for George to think he should be told about what had gone down. But, then again, why wouldn't Harper want this Jason character to know?

'I figured that since my vocal cords are in excellent working order I should be the one to phone him and say you're all right,' George continued as though Harper hadn't glared hard enough to poleaxe him.

Harper sighed as she lifted her hands in resignation. 'You're right. But no drama, okay?'

The man grunted. 'What are the chances?'

'None,' Harper muttered as Karin rushed up to engulf her in a hug.

'Hey, Harper, you poor thing. I couldn't believe my eyes when I came out of the treatment room and saw that man holding a gun to your head.' She raised watery eyes to Cody. 'I'm glad you saved her.'

Saved her was a stretch of the truth. But he was pleased he'd been able to take Lowlife down before he'd hurt their doctor any more than he already had. He really hated seeing people get hurt, and he particularly hadn't wanted to see anything happen to Harper. 'Thanks for the vote of confidence,' he drawled. 'But Harper saved herself. She started the ball rolling when she dropped to the floor.' His relief at Harper being safe was overwhelming. Today the outcome had been good. He wouldn't think back to the darkest day of his life— not now. Too disturbing.

They were still standing in the middle of the department while other doctors and nurses were ducking and diving around them now, bringing patients in from the waiting room. Cody had had about all he could take of people staring at him and clapping him on the back for doing a cracking job on the assailant. They meant well, but they had no idea what it had really been like in Resus One. 'Come on, Doc, let's get out of everyone's way. Go have that coffee George mentioned.'

'Doc?' Harper shivered. That annoyance with George transferred to him. 'That man called me "Doc".'

Comprehension slammed him. Of course, Lowlife had, and in a denigrating tone at that. 'I'm sorry, never thought about it.' He didn't want to rile her any more. Not after what they'd been through together.

Her shoulders drooped momentarily, then tightened again as she drew a long, slow breath. 'Thank you for knocking him down. I am grateful. You could've been shot.' Unbelievably her eyes teared up. Again. For him? Not likely.

He'd never have picked her for the weepy sort, but then today hadn't been exactly normal. Violence undermined the strongest of people. Even his gut had tightened painfully at the moment when that gun had appeared. 'Stop talking and give your throat a rest.' He reached to take her elbow, saw those watery eyes widen and dropped his hand. Of course he was out of line, even if he'd only wanted to help. Being overly friendly to a colleague at work, no matter how well intentioned, could be seen as overstepping the mark. Apparently that hug had been okay at the time but now any other move from him wouldn't be.

Harper muttered, 'I've seen violence in the ED heaps of times.'

'But never directed specifically at you, I bet.' The thought of that kind of personal, immediate threat brought back unpleasant memories. The looks on the faces of women in the pubs when their men came home from a dry six-week stint on the fishing trawlers. Some of the crew over-indulged in alcohol and drugs, then took the resultant mood swings out on their partners. He'd stopped going to the pub with the guys after a while, unable to cope with what he saw but never managing to prevent it. He'd tried talking them out of their rages, had taken some punches and given a few back in self-defence, but he'd never convinced those guys that what they were doing to their women was wrong.

Some men had a mind-set about using their fists that was impossible to change.

But that was then, and he'd moved on to a different world, or so he'd thought. 'Come on. George's office will be a lot quieter. Even with the police joining us.'

Her fingers worked her forehead, then her temples. 'You're right.'

'Are you okay? Apart from your neck and throat being squashed?' She looked paler than before. Shock would do that, though he thought something else might be going on.

'Of course I am,' she snapped and stormed towards the corridor that'd take them to the office affectionately known as George's cave. But at the door she stopped and graced him with a wobbly smile. 'Why wouldn't I be? It's not every day there's so much excitement in the department.'

'There's something we can be grateful for.' The fact that the man had held that gun to a doctor's head put today's example of crazy way up there on the scale of craziness. Apparently Harper hadn't seen as much of the rougher side of humanity in her working life as some medics in big city hospitals did.

'To think this is Wellington, not Los Angeles, where there are permanent armed guards on the doors.' For someone who shouldn't be talking too much, she was doing an awful lot of it. A reaction to everything that had gone down?

'You've worked in LA?' If she wasn't going to be quiet then a change of subject might be for the best about now. For both of them. Now that the showdown was over the adrenaline had backed off, leaving him feeling shaky, despite his previous experience with out-of-control thugs.

'No. Never. But I know people who have.' Then she turned the questions on him. 'I know nothing about you. Where were you working before starting here?'

'Invercargill. I did my training there and stayed on working in the emergency department for another year.'

'That suggests you're a late starter.'

Way past being wet behind the ears, for sure. Cody shrugged. 'I had a career change at twenty-seven.'

'From what?'

'Commercial fishing.'

'You're kidding me!' Surprise tainted her eyes.

He was used to that. Fisherman to nurse took a bit of getting around for most people. 'I've found my niche.'

Nudging her into the office, he closed the door to keep the noise of the department out and instantly wished he hadn't. The room wasn't much bigger than a shoebox and somehow this woman with all her questions seemed to fill it so that he couldn't put enough space between them. A scent of lemon or lime wafted in the air, reminding him of summer days in his grandfather's orchard. The days when he'd been young, carefree and a little hellion. A long time ago.

'Why Wellington?' She blushed. 'Sorry, none of my business, and not relative to the job.'

None of your questions are. But suddenly he couldn't shut up either. 'I'm originally from Kelburn.' *Yes, just along the road from the hospital.* 'My mum's still here and my brother has a home in Central Wellington, though he's currently working in Sydney at the General Hospital.'

'Medicine runs in the family then?'

He pulled out a chair for her and tamped down the jerk of annoyance at her surprise. He might be a big man but he had the manners of a gentleman. Except when it came to dealing with thugs. 'My brother's an orthopaedic surgeon. Our father was a GP. Mother was a nurse. And so am I.' And darned proud of it. It beat fishing out in the middle of the wild ocean any day, or trying to straighten out dumb jerks who thought the world owed them. Though that had caught up with him here this morning. Once again.

A brief knock on the door and two cops pushed into the room, filling the remaining space, which brought him closer to Harper.

'Statement time,' said the younger one as she gave him the once-over—a slow, 'I like what I'm seeing' once-over that stroked his ego but didn't have his brain wanting to follow up. Nor his body.

Pulling out another chair, he copped a smirk from Harper. So she'd seen the constable's appraisal. He shrugged. Nothing he could do about it; he hadn't asked for it. It just happened. He turned to the other police officer. 'You want to ask more questions? Or just take statements?'

The sooner this was done and that coffee arrived, then the sooner he could go back to work and put the morning behind him. That was if George let them go back to work. He seemed pretty adamant that they were going to have to go home for the rest of the day and rest up. Matilda and Jess too. Harper wasn't going to like that; he was sure of it.

When they were done with the police Harper pulled out her phone and checked her messages. 'Who doesn't know what happened?' she muttered and shut it off completely without answering any texts or emails.

Cody had texted his brother earlier to say he was good and not to worry about him. They'd talk tonight. Maybe. 'You're not putting it out there that you're fine?'

She seemed very reluctant to talk to her family or this Jason character.

'George did it.' Her mouth lifted slightly. 'He never does take any notice of what I want. No wonder he's friends with my brothers.'

Cody thought she was just as guilty of that after George examined Harper's throat and tried to make her take the rest of the shift off. Of course she refused, flouncing out to the department and picking up the next file on the way to the waiting room. George wasn't best pleased, but he relented in the end. They could stay to the end of the shift but were relegated to paperwork only.

'I'm fine, George,' Harper insisted with a scowl.

'You might think so, Harper, but you've had a huge shock. I'm not comfortable with you treating patients till you've had a full night's sleep. That's non-negotiable.'

Cody actually wouldn't have minded knocking off early for the day but he didn't want to leave Harper alone after what they'd been through. He felt weirdly protective of her after all the bravery she'd shown. She was quite a woman.

Careful, Cody. That way lies trouble.

'You feel like going for a drink?' Cody asked Harper at the end of their shift as they pushed through the swing doors and out into the corridor. 'We've certainly earned one today.' The rest of the shift was already at the pub just down the road, no doubt yacking about the event that had overtaken the department that morning, which kind of had him regretting his suggestion to Harper. He'd had enough of the talk. Already the truth had been expanded, the resultant stories getting way out of control.

'I don't think so.' She looked decidedly uncomfortable with the idea. Or was that about going with him?

His tongue got the better of him, as it was prone to do at the most inconvenient of times. 'You don't drink with your colleagues?' She wouldn't now, not if he was going to be there.

'I don't drink at all when I have a migraine.'

He swore. Now he knew why she kept rubbing her temples. 'How're you getting home?' he asked as he saw her blink furiously when they stepped out into the blinding summer sun.

'I have a car.' Her chin jutted out. 'How about you?'

'I have a motorbike.'

'Then you're not asking me for a ride home?'

'No, but I am offering to drive you home in your car. You are in no fit state to be behind the wheel.'

'Yes, nurse.' Her tone would've sounded sarcastic if there hadn't been resignation and tiredness lacing her words. It seemed as though now she'd stopped work she was unravelling completely. Her eyes were half-closed, and she dug around in her bag and dragged out sunglasses, which she slapped on her face before heading towards the staff car park.

He followed. 'You know I'm right. A migraine is hell, apparently. Do you get blackouts with yours?'

Her mouth tightened and she said nothing.

'Toss in that bruised and swollen throat, the shock of being held hostage, and you're in need of a little pampering.' Was he offering to pamper her? No, that had come out all wrong. But he was damned if he was going to retract his statement. He didn't do being caught on the back foot—not by attractive, sharp-tongued women, at any rate.

Harper ducked between vehicles, seemingly intent on the furthest row. When she reached a dazzling blue, high-performance car she pinged the locks and glared at him over the roof. 'Forgot where you parked your motorbike?'

Cody ignored her anger, believing it probably wasn't really directed at him but more at the situation she found herself in. He wanted to help her, be there for her, and knew better than to come out and say so. He tried another tack. Running his hand over the bonnet, he noted, 'Nice. Bet it goes like a cut cat.'

'Faster.' There was the smallest twist of her lips and a hint of laughter in the pained eyes she exposed when she removed her sunglasses to rub her temples again.

So heat did run along her veins. Not often, maybe, but obviously sometimes. Now, there was a challenge. She was into fast cars. But not today. He stared at her and held out his hand.

Harper stared straight back. At least, she tried to, but that migraine must've got the better of her because she blinked and her chin dropped. The keys sailed through the air and he snatched them before they landed on the paintwork. 'Careful.' Opening the passenger door, he waited patiently for her to come round and slide inside then, closing her door, he headed for the other side of the car, whistling under his breath.

Miss—was she a Miss, or a Mrs?—*Dr* White could be a pain in the backside. But she was also magnificent. He could appreciate the details without being tempted to learn more about her. If it hadn't been for the day's drama he wouldn't be regarding her twice. He wouldn't know that she had soft, muscle-tightening curves in all the right places. Or that she smelt delicious. She was clearly intelligent, and was a superb doctor. She was starting to sound too good. *Harper's nothing to me in any way other than as a colleague.*

Anyway, she had a Jason in her life.

* * *

Harper leaned her head back against the headrest and groaned. Talk about the day from hell. All she wanted was to crawl into bed in her blacked-out room and let the headache drugs that she would take now she'd finished work do their magic. Hopefully she'd sleep, and not have nightmares about that gun or the man wielding it.

'Address?' Cody asked.

Without opening her eyes, she rattled off the street and number, then sighed with relief when he said he knew where to go. Talking hurt, and if she didn't have to utter another word till next week she'd be happy. Not that she'd kept quiet earlier. It was like something had got hold of her tongue, had had her blathering away like she didn't know how to stop, even though her throat protested every syllable. Why had she asked Cody all those personal questions? It wasn't as though she had to have the answers to be able to work with him.

But after everything that had happened she'd felt a need to know more about the man who'd come to her rescue, who'd been there throughout the whole ordeal, who'd even understood her sorrow at losing her patient. He'd surprised her with how recently he'd qualified. She'd done the sums—he was in his early thirties. Fishermen had to be tough, physically and mentally, to cope with the conditions they worked in. She'd seen that in Cody today, and she'd also noticed the soft streak that made him so popular with patients.

Cody had stepped up, tried to talk the gunman into letting her go and hadn't hesitated to take him down when she'd deliberately dropped towards the floor. It had been a risk doing that but she'd felt Cody was a part of her, that he'd known what was going on in her head all the time. The way he'd reacted suggested he'd dealt with villains before. Intriguing. But nothing to do with her. Whatever Cody had done in the past, she did not need to know. That would be getting too personal, and there was no point in doing that when she had no intention of socialising with him outside work.

Cody interrupted her thoughts. 'You fixed for pills for that migraine?'

'Yes.' Like a doctor wouldn't be prepared when she had regular migraines. 'Of course.'

'Just checking. You want anything for home? Food, milk or bottled water? I can duck into the supermarket for you.'

'Got everything I need.' *Except a loving man.* She gasped. Where had that come from? Had that crack on her skull with the gun addled her brain? Not once since she'd packed her bags and walked out the front door of the house she'd shared with Darren had she believed she was ready for a relationship with another man. A quick fling, yes—anything deep and meaningful, no. If there was even a man out there who'd accept her infertility issue, she'd struggle to believe he wouldn't change his mind like Darren had done. She'd just have to wait until she was fifty and beyond wanting to be a mother before getting involved with someone.

Her gaze slid sideways to study the profile of the man next to her. He looked good behind the wheel in this big car. Strong, easy in his body, confident. Then there was his reliability—as far as she'd seen, anyway—and his friendly, caring side. There was that perfectionist element she'd noted before the morning had gone pear-shaped, but perfectionism could be a fault or a good trait. He could also get angry, as witnessed with their assailant. Controlled anger though, not a rant or rage.

'You're staring.'

She was. And liking what she saw more and more. A big enough reason to close her eyes again. Which she did, and sank further down the seat. Thank goodness for Fridays. The coming weekend would give her time to recover fully from the migraine. Whether she'd stop shaking from shock every time she thought about what had gone down in the ED by Monday was another story. What if the assailant *had* fired his gun? Had wounded someone—Jess, Cody or her? She shivered abruptly.

He placed one hand on her thigh, squeezed lightly and removed his hand fast. 'Don't think about him. It's over now.' He sounded so darned calm, as though nothing had affected him.

Yet his ability to constantly know what she was thinking riled her for no real reason. Again she pictured him taking that man down and her mood swiftly softened. He was very confident and for a large man he'd moved fast, light on his feet. The assailant hadn't known what had hit him. Which was just as well, or it might've been Cody feeling the hot end of that gun. She shivered. For some strange reason she took real comfort from his confidence and was inordinately grateful to him for how he'd dealt with the situation. Also for his tenderness in that hug. Confused. That was what she was.

Nausea swamped her senses. She was going to be sick. No, she wasn't. Not in front of Cody, nurse or not. That would be the final straw in a very bad day. Pressing the switch to lower her window, she leaned over and relished the air flowing across her face. It wasn't cold air, but at least cooler than what was inside the car. No doubt she'd look a right state by the time they reached home, but at this moment she couldn't care less.

'You need to stop?' Cody asked, already slowing the car and easing closer to the edge of the road.

'No. Keep going.' The sooner she got home, the better. The blinding pain behind her eyes was increasing in intensity, but at least the nausea was sort of under control. This was becoming the migraine to beat all migraines in her experience, no doubt exacerbated by the tension from earlier.

Her apartment was just around the corner. Soon she'd be shot of Cody Brand. Until Monday and work. With a bit of luck, by then they'd be back to being a doctor and a nurse working in the same department. Hopefully by then all the talk and texts would've died down too. She didn't fancy multiple reruns of today's event.

'There's a car in your driveway.' Cody's voice was deeper than most men's, yet it soothed her frayed nerves and battered mind. 'Want me to park on the road?'

'Great.' She'd forgotten about Gemma calling in after her shopping expedition so they could have a wine together. Not happening now; the mere thought of wine turned her stomach. 'That'd be fine. I'll shift the car later.' Tomorrow when she finally crawled out of bed.

Harper was hardly aware of Cody pulling up. He had her door open and was reaching for her elbow so quickly it came as a surprise. 'Come on. I'll see you to your door.'

'I can manage.' And she promptly proved herself wrong when her knees refused to hold her upright.

'Now, don't take this the wrong way,' Cody murmured as he swung her up in his arms and nudged the door shut with his hip. 'But falling flat on your face after everything else could really mess up your day.' He strode up the path towards her front door as though she was no heavier than a bag of spuds. A very small bag at that.

Harper didn't bother arguing. He wouldn't listen and she didn't have any energy left. Besides, it was lovely lying against that expansive chest and feeling strong arms around her. Arms she imagined holding her through the night. *Jeez, Harper, get a grip.*

'Harper? Jason said you were all right but you're not looking great.' Typical Gemma: go for the throat. *No, someone else already did that today.*

'Gemma,' she squeaked.

Her sister-in-law stood in the doorway, her eyes flicking between her and Cody, worry slowly turning to speculation as she studied Cody from head to foot. 'Or do I need to grab my bag and head away pronto? Leave you two alone?'

Harper cringed. She loved Gemma to bits but the woman had a mission in life to find her a man who'd accept all her problems without batting an eyelid—and from what she was reading on Gemma's face right this minute Cody was a prime target. No way in hell. Squirming out of Cody's arms, she stood shakily between him and Gemma. 'I've got a migraine.'

It seemed Gemma had become deaf overnight. She focused entirely on Cody and asked, 'Who are you?'

'I'm Cody. I work with Harper.'

Feeling Cody's hand on her elbow—again—Harper wanted to shrug him away but doubted she had the strength to walk unaided. 'I need to lie down. Going to take a rain check on that wine, Gem.'

'Your voice's all weird.' Gemma leaned closer. 'What's wrong with your neck? Jason told me about the gunman but you've been hurt. You're not all right, are you? That's why Cody's here.'

'Harper needs to get inside and lie down in a dark room.' Cody was firm, like he'd take no argument.

Gemma caught the message and led the way indoors. 'What really happened, Harper? Spill.'

'I— There—' Her throat closed over and tears filled her eyes. She raised her head, caught Cody's gaze and nodded at him.

'You want me to explain?'

Once again, Cody to the rescue. This was getting out of hand, but she dipped her head. Words were beyond her. Accepting help from any one didn't feature in her everyday life. Not even her overly protective brothers got a chance very often. But today, right now, she was all out of helping herself.

Cody told Gemma, 'Let's put Harper to bed first.' That was the most important thing to do. The whys and wherefores of the situation could wait a few more minutes. He smiled to himself with relief. At least this woman could help Harper out of her clothes while he hung out in the kitchen. He would not be disappointed at missing out on that treat.

Really? Really. Getting too close and personal with Harper was the last thing he needed. He had a feeling that getting to know her at all would undermine the defences he'd pulled around himself the day Sadie had died. The agony over his loss, the sense of failure and guilt, had taken many dark days and months to quieten enough for him to start moving forward, one tiny step at a time. He wasn't going to risk going back there again.

'I'm taking you home with me.' Gemma's hands were on her hips as she watched Harper gingerly sit down on her bed.

Harper shook her head but didn't open her eyes. She was probably beyond dealing with anything right now.

So Cody stepped into the gap. 'Harper's better off staying here, unless you live next door. She's not in good shape.' *There's absolutely nothing wrong with her shape.* Cody closed his eyes and dragged up some patience with himself. Then, looking at Gemma, he explained about the guy who'd caused all the trouble. 'Her throat's swollen and painful, and the whole event has been a huge shock. I don't know if the migraine had begun before that lowlife did his number on her, or it's a result of his actions, but it's a bad one.'

Gemma's face paled. 'You can't stay here after that. What would Jason say if I arrived home without you? I know it will be uncomfortable on the drive but you're coming home to the bay for the weekend.'

Harper's eyes flew open. 'But—'

'But nothing. I'll pack some clothes and we'll be on our way.' She spun around and stuck a hand out at Cody. 'No wonder she didn't introduce us properly. Gemma White, married to Harper's oldest brother, Jason. Thanks for taking care of her. One more thing, can you carry her out to my car when I've collected a few things?'

So that was who Jason was. Unexpected relief rolled through Cody. Not her husband or partner, but her brother. George must be pally with him if he'd wanted to tell him about what had happened to his sister. 'I hate to point this out but I don't think Harper's up to going anywhere.'

Harper lifted grateful eyes in his direction. She was definitely all out of energy. Exhaustion and pain filled her mesmerising gaze. Her body was slumped in a loose heap on the edge of the bed and he doubted her ability even to lift her legs up under the sheet. He couldn't take his eyes off her as she looked up at him.

But it was the sadness in that gaze that caused him to make a fool of himself. 'I'll stay here the night, keep an eye on you.' He nodded at Harper, who now stared at him, a mix of gratitude and horror further darkening those eyes.

Gemma nodded. 'That's a perfect solution. I take it you're a doctor, since you work with Harper?'

'Not a doctor. A nurse.'

Which was totally the wrong thing to tell this woman because she clapped her hands. 'Even better. A nurse is exactly what Harper needs. Right, I'll get you undressed and into bed, my girl, then leave you in the capable hands of Nurse Cody. He'll be able to sleep in the kids' room. Just as well I changed the sheets on the beds earlier while I was waiting for you to come home. That couch in the lounge may be big but not big enough for his bod.'

'Jeez, woman, do you ever come up for air?' Cody asked Gemma with a grin and was rewarded with a startled gasp of laughter from the bed where Harper had finally stopped staring at him. 'What?' he demanded. These ladies were full-on.

'I could get to like you,' Harper gasped in her new croaky voice.

That'd be good. No, it wouldn't. 'We'll see,' he answered airily, then made the mistake of glancing at Gemma and sucked in a sharp breath.

Her expression spelled mischief. Lots of it. 'This just gets better and better,' she murmured.

'Gemma.' Even with her swollen throat and feeling like hell it was obvious Harper was not pleased with her sister-in-law.

'Right, let's get you into bed so you can sleep off this migraine. Where are your tablets?' Gemma was already opening a drawer and pulling out some cotton night-dress thing that she held up with distaste. 'You don't listen to anything I tell you, do you, sis?'

Cody headed for the door. He wasn't hanging around while Harper removed her work clothes and slipped into that hideous yellow-and-pink-striped concoction. At least he agreed with Gemma on something. 'I'll get some water so you can take your tablets,' he called over his shoulder.

Ten minutes later, Gemma joined him in the kitchen. 'I hope you haven't got any plans for Sunday after-noon, because it's Jason's birthday, and Harper needs to be with us. The Whites are big on family stuff, you know? The brothers—' she wriggled her forefingers in the air between them '—will want to meet the man who looked out for her today. You must stay for lunch and the cricket.'

'Cricket?' he asked. What was this woman on about?

'You know—bat, ball and wickets. The kids can't get enough of it. Bet when you hit a ball it stays hit.'

'It's been a while since I swung a bat.' He shook his head. 'Thanks for the invitation, Gemma, but don't count me in. I've already got something on.'

'You sure? We have a lot of fun, there's always great food and—' she grinned '—ice-cold beer.'

Cody gave her a smile in return. 'Thanks, but no thanks.' Harper wouldn't be pleased if he accepted the invitation, however graciously it had been extended. They worked together; playing together wasn't part of the deal. He headed to the bedroom with Harper's water glass in his hand.

'Gemma giving you a hard time?' Harper asked as he handed her the glass.

Knowing Harper would back him all the way about not joining her family, he grunted, 'She insists I join you all for the birthday do on Sunday.'

'Oh.' She winced as she swallowed the pills. 'You'd have to stay all afternoon.'

What happened to her seeing things his way? 'I've got plans to spend the afternoon with my mother.' It was what he did in the weekends now that he was back in town. Her condition had lost her most of her friends and she was lonely.

'Bring her with you, with us.'

Yeah, right. 'Sorry, no can do. Mum's got dementia and needs watching all the time.' Not to mention how rattled she got when out of her usual haunts or was with people she'd never met.

'Well, you know best, of course. But there are plenty of us to keep an eye on her. She might have fun! The kids will be friendly. My parents and brothers and sister are quite nice most of the time. The brothers and sisters-in-law are housetrained on a good day.'

'I thought it hurt to talk.' He was over these bossy women. 'You sure you and Gemma aren't sisters, rather than related by marriage?' They had the same genes.

Harper grimaced. 'We'll talk some more tomorrow.'

That was it? She must be feeling even worse than he'd thought. 'Go to sleep,' he growled and strode out into the kitchen, where thankfully Gemma was waiting with keys in hand, ready to take flight.

'Thanks for doing this.' She grinned and stretched up on tiptoes to drop a sisterly kiss on his chin. 'I really appreciate it. Her brothers will be more than thankful.

Harper can be very stubborn at times and I know she'd never have come home with me tonight.'

'I must be stark, raving mad,' Cody muttered as the front door closed behind her. Outmanoeuvred was what he really was. It didn't sit comfortably. Not at all.

CHAPTER THREE

NOW WHAT WAS he supposed to do? Nearly five in the afternoon, a beautiful woman hopefully sound asleep in the room next door—which was not how he usually spent time with women in their homes—and he had absolutely nothing to do. He was not going to check up on Harper. What if she was awake? Or, worse, woke while he was in her room? She'd be calling him a pervert at the very least.

Staring around, he took in the multitude of framed photos hanging on the walls and standing on bookcases and the sideboard. They were mostly of kids, boys and girls—very young, middling and nearly teenaged, he guessed. Laughing, smiling, pulling faces, dressed in school uniforms, in shorts and shirts, ski outfits, swimming gear and playing cricket. Basically all about having fun. With Harper right amongst them—laughing and smiling. Cute, and nothing like the serious woman who kept everyone in the department on their toes as she worked alongside them.

The kids' room was where he was supposed to sleep tonight. So, Harper had children. Where were they? And where was their dad? He obviously wasn't Jason. Why hadn't Harper wanted her brother to know what had happened at work today? And where did George fit in?

Questions tumbled over and over in his brain, cranking up his agitation. It irked him he didn't know these things about Harper.

It really riled him that he wanted to find out.

Cody's chuckle was bitter. He'd loved Sadie deeply, and her death had made him wary of being so vulnerable again. Even nearly five years down the track he couldn't look back at those dark days without curling in on himself. Sure, he'd love a family, had bought a house suited for one, but to step up and take a chance? He was so not ready. The day might come when he was, but today wasn't it. He sighed. Nor was tomorrow.

Cody pushed the past aside and took another scan of the photos. No man seemed to be especially close with Harper, as in 'in a relationship' close. There were two men hugging her and some kids in many of the photos. Presumably one was Jason. The other could be another brother. Both guys were holding women with love written all over their faces, Gemma being one of them. So was Harper single or not? In any relationship? Divorced? There were those kids who apparently used the spare room, so there had to be a father out there, which meant a man in Harper's life in one way or another.

Harper's bedroom hadn't looked as though she shared it with anyone. It was too feminine, and not one item of clothing was male, there was no comb or shaver on the dresser, or the bits and pieces he'd expect on the bedside table on the opposite side of the bed to the one Harper had crawled into.

The mystery was no clearer in the second, tiny bedroom where two single beds with bright quilts, one with fire engines and the other with frogs printed all over them, took up most of the space. More photos were interspersed with pictures of everything from lions to

TV cartoon characters. Hell, he'd be having nightmares sleeping in here.

He *was* meant to be sleeping in here.

He might check out that couch. Except it was only a two-seater and he was six-five tall. Even these beds weren't going to be long enough but he'd be able to manoeuvre himself into a more comfortable position in one than on the couch.

On his hip his phone vibrated, giving him a much-needed diversion, though he didn't recognise the number on the screen. 'Yup?'

'Now I know you're definitely back in town.'

He recognised the voice of his old mate instantly, despite not having talked for years. 'Hey, Trent, been meaning to catch up, but got busy, you know?' Truth was he'd been reluctant to get in touch because he was uncertain of the welcome he'd get. At sixteen they'd been the closest of mates at school and into loads of mischief, but the day school had finished he'd headed out the gate without a backward glance, leaving everything and everyone behind.

Including Trent. Eager to get on with life, rebelling against settling into more study, this time at university, he'd put his surprisingly not-too-bad exam results aside and found a job down south on a fishing trawler. Despite only being seventeen, he'd already had the body of a rugby prop, so getting a job had been easy in an industry that required plenty of muscle.

'Police Inspector Trent Ballinger to you.' A deep laugh rumbled through the phone.

'Way to go, man. Well done, you.' Cody headed for the lounge and the garden on the other side of the sliding glass doors. He didn't want to wake Harper, and anyway he needed some fresh air after being holed up with her in the car and then here. Hell, even her home smelt of citrus, a scent he was rapidly accepting as Harper's scent.

'Saw your name on the report that was filed a few hours ago about Strong and his mule. It wasn't hard to track you down.'

His friend did have the New Zealand police resources on his side. 'That lowlife locked up good and tight?'

'You should've given him what for while you had the opportunity.' Trent sighed. 'I didn't say that. But, hell, the man hasn't stopped whinging since the boys brought him in. Anyone would think he'd been hard done by, losing those drugs.'

'It was tempting to give him a wee nudge.' He was not admitting to the knee slam in the lowlife's back, though. Trent might still be a friend but he was a cop first and foremost. 'How did Strong get in on the act in the first place? I presume he was waiting to pick up Frew outside the international terminal but he managed to slip into our department too easily. I wouldn't have thought the paramedics would've let him ride in with them.'

'He followed them, and strolled up to the ambulance bay as they were disembarking, waved a card that the paramedics believed was a police identity and walked on in.'

'Guess if you've got the balls you can get away with just about anything.' Cody was shocked at how simple it had been, and a tad angry.

'More like if you've got a loaded gun you can get away with most things.'

Cody swallowed. 'It *was* loaded?' After flipping out of Lowlife's hand, it'd spun across the floor to be picked up by Harper, who'd then stuck it under her waistband before attending to Frew. He shivered. Maybe luck had been on their side after all. 'I thought it might be but hoped I was wrong.'

'I think you'll find the hospital will be tightening security quick-fast,' Trent said.

'The old stable door trick.' It wasn't right that outsiders, detectives or not, could get in so easily. During the night no one got through, but it seemed daytime security was lax. 'From what I've seen of George Sampson so far, he'll already have someone looking into it.'

'How's the doc? She holding up?'

Cody chuckled. 'You always ask this many questions?'

'Occupational hazard,' Trent replied. 'You avoiding the question?'

No, he didn't want to talk about Harper, not even to a long lost, now found friend. Somehow talking about her felt like he was going behind her back, which made no sense whatsoever. He went with the medical. 'Her throat and neck are very sore but otherwise she's physically okay. Apart from a migraine that's knocked her to her knees,' he added in case Trent's lot wanted to question her some more today.

'Stress will do that.'

Cody got an image in his skull of that gun being held to Harper's head, and the rank fear pervading her sweet eyes. 'Not sure how she'll go with all the head stuff, though. It'll be tough trying to put aside the fact that someone threatened to shoot her brains out.'

'I hear she handled the situation well,' Trent said, then thankfully changed the subject. 'How long have you been back in town?'

He winced, regretting not phoning Trent sooner. 'Six weeks. Shifted Mother into a retirement home with hospital facilities and then packed up her house, sold off stuff, all of the usual.' It had been hard going through forty years of her possessions. She'd kept everything of his dad's since he'd died ten years back as well, including all his clothes, even his old pipes that he'd smoked in the evenings and the rods from trout-fishing excursions. The rods which were now in *his* shed in case one day he had a child he could take on similar forays. If he ever got brave enough to start over.

The trip down memory lane had at times made him laugh, and at others caused him to shed tears for the mum and dad he'd loved. Still loved. His mother mightn't be the same any more, with the dementia doing its number on her, but she was still Mother. Packing up everything and getting rid of most of the clutter had reminded him of fun family holidays to the beach when he'd been small, and of annoying the hell out of his older brother just because he could.

'So, you up for a pint?' Trent asked, reminding Cody he was in the middle of a conversation. 'I'm done for the day.'

He'd kill for one. 'I can't tonight. Got something on.'

'Found a hot female, huh?'

'Nah, haven't got time for that at the moment.' Stretching the truth wasn't a lie. Harper wasn't his type of woman; she was too focused on her career from what he'd seen, and obviously with family issues which she wouldn't want him getting involved in. *But she is hot. Sizzling.* He was seeing that more and more the longer he spent in her company.

'I heard about your wife.'

Who hadn't? It'd been headline news for days. 'It's history now.' Except the consequence was he didn't talk about personal things or want to put his heart on the line again. He knew the doctors had done everything they could to save her. It didn't make him feel any better.

'That when you took up nursing?' Trent had known he'd considered it, even at school.

'Yep. It was horrible not being able to help Sadie.' Huh? He didn't do talking, remember? It had to be the day that had screwed his brain.

'You back home for good?'

Cody managed a chuckle. 'I've bought myself a house that needs lots of work, a big sucker on the hill overlooking Oriental Bay. It's going to keep me out of mischief for years, so yes, I guess I'm here for the long haul.'

'You staying out of mischief? I must be talking to the wrong Cody Brand.'

If only he knew. Knowing he was stuck in this apartment tonight with a woman he'd only met five days ago, and who he was now babysitting, would bring Trent to his knees with laughter. As Cody stuffed his phone in his back pocket, he wondered just what was stopping him walking out and going to pick up his motorbike before heading down to the pub for that drink with Trent.

A promise that he'd stay the night.

A sense that Harper needed someone to keep an eye out for her. He always knew when someone wanted that—just didn't always do it right. But he kept on trying.

Cody *wanted* to be here, making sure Harper got through the night without any nightmares about what might've happened if everything had gone wrong.

And if that migraine got worse he wanted to take care of her.

It had to be the nurse in him coming out. He couldn't think of any other reason for letting his caring side get the better of him in this case. It wasn't as though Harper needed protecting from her would-be assailant. The guy was behind bars, for now at least.

But he couldn't help the memories creeping in as he twisted a cap off a lonely bottle of beer he found in the fridge. Looking out for Harper today had been instinctive, and easy. He'd have done whatever it took to get that man away from her. Now he'd do everything possible to keep on his guard with Dr White. Someone had to look out for his heart, and that someone was him.

Harper woke slowly. There was a vice around her head and drums behind her eyes. Her stomach ached, as did her throat.

But that was nothing compared to the film reeling through her mind, bringing into sharp focus the man with his gun and how he'd held it to her head.

At least she'd woken up before the pictures had got too violent. But now she didn't want to go back to sleep—not yet, anyway. She was shaking. How close had Strong come to killing her?

'Stop it,' she yelled at herself. Doing this wasn't helping at all. She had to be tough, put it all behind her.

Her mouth was dry. Reaching for the glass on the bedside table, she was disappointed to find it empty. She'd have to move.

Another tablet for her migraine wouldn't go amiss. What time had she taken the last one? Pushing up onto an elbow, she paused until the room steadied. Light streamed down the hall. Had she left the kitchen light on earlier? Or the one in the lounge? No recollection of being in those rooms came to her, but that didn't bother her. It wasn't unusual for her to drop into a deep sleep after taking the migraine meds.

Carefully sitting up and putting her feet on the floor,

she once again waited for her head to catch up with the rest of her body. The headache had calmed down a little. Or was it waiting to pounce when she went out into the light?

Cody Brand. His name slammed into her head.

He was in her apartment somewhere. Sleeping in the kids' room? Or sitting in the lounge watching television?

It all rushed in, setting her head spinning harder. Gemma being bossy. Cody saying he'd stay the night to keep an eye on her. He was why she'd fallen asleep so quickly, all fear of being attacked again allayed by his presence.

Most of all she recalled being held in strong arms against a broad, warm chest and wanting to snuggle even closer as he'd carried her up the drive. He'd made her feel safe so often throughout the day. There were a few other things he had made her feel too that she'd prefer not to go into.

Oozing a stalled breath over her lips, she debated crawling back under the sheet and pretending she hadn't woken up. But the pounding in her head and the tightening of that band of pain wasn't going away if she didn't have another tablet. And some water. She was so thirsty her tongue was sticking to the roof of her mouth.

Standing on unsteady legs, she aimed for the kitchen, hoping she wouldn't find Cody in there. The last thing she wanted was for him to see her in her nightie, but searching for the robe that she rarely used somewhere at the back of her wardrobe would expend energy she didn't have. She just wanted the tablet and water and to climb back into bed.

The kitchen was empty, but the TV was on in the lounge with the sound muted. Harper couldn't resist. She peeked around the corner and gasped. That big body was sprawled over her couch with the neighbour's cat curled on top of the chest she'd enjoyed so much. Her heart flipped. Cute. Who'd have thought it of such a large man? A gentle rumble erupted. Cody was sound asleep, snoring softly.

On the floor sat a takeout pizza box with two pieces left. Was she hungry? Stepping closer she bent down to steal a piece but got a whiff of cold melted cheese and something else unpleasant. Her stomach immediately protested. Fair enough. She didn't usually eat during a migraine episode.

Straightening up, she studied Cody. Stubble had appeared on his chin. What would that feel like against the palm of her hand?

She'd never know. Gripping her hands together in case she gave into the need crawling through her, she backed away.

Of course she didn't have eyes in the back of her head. Duh. Thump. The back of her leg banged into the coffee table and she sat down heavily on it. Of course the table shouldn't have been there in the first place. Who'd shifted it? Her eyes went straight to the man now waking up on her couch.

'Hey, you're up.' Cody stretched, carefully lifted the cat off and placed it on what little piece of couch he wasn't taking up. Then he sat up and Harper felt dwarfed. Not that she was tiny.

'I'm getting some water and going back to bed.'

'Want anything to eat?' He glanced at the pizza box and looked back to her. 'I can scramble an egg, if you like.'

Since shaking her head hurt worse than talking through her bruised throat, she said, 'No, thanks.' But she didn't move. Sitting here was easier than getting up.

'How are you feeling now?'

Spreading her fingers on her right hand she tipped her hand back and forth. 'So, so.'

'Going back to bed? Or staying up for a while? I'll change the TV channel. Cricket's over, anyway.'

'No. The flickering light would aggravate my migraine. What's the time?'

A glance at his watch. 'Ten-forty.' He stood up, stretching that long body no doubt to ease the kinks gained from lying on the couch. 'I'll get your water and tablets.'

She didn't need him running round after her. At the same time she couldn't find the strength to stand up and go get what she needed. 'Okay,' she muttered to his back as he strolled out to the kitchen, looking for all the world like he was used to being in her home.

Actually, he looked comfortable in here, like he belonged. He and the cat. Glancing sideways, she knew immediately how Puss had got inside. Cool air flowed in through the open glass doors and an empty beer bottle stood on the concrete by the barbecue table. He'd made himself at home, and Harper wasn't sure how she felt about that.

'Here you go.' A large hand with a glass and pill bottle appeared in front of her. 'Get those into you.' He sat down again. 'Some guy phoned about tennis tomorrow. Something about playing an inter-club match.'

She shook her head. 'You must've got it wrong. I can barely hit the ball over the net yet.'

'You're learning to play?'

'Uh-huh. I'm trying to learn to play. Who'd have thought it would be so hard to bang a ball across a net?' She'd joined the local club in spring and wouldn't be renewing her membership at the end of the season. In fact, she doubted she'd even go to club day again. 'What did you tell him?'

'It wasn't my place to say anything other than you'd phone tomorrow, though I sort of indicated you might be indisposed.'

'Define "sort of".' He'd surprised her. Most people wouldn't think twice about saying she was in bed with a migraine, or worse, describe the attack in the ED that morning.

'Said you had rehearsals for the Christmas ballet in town. He was a little surprised—apparently you're not very nimble on your feet.' Those spring-green eyes were twinkling at her.

'Look.' She lifted the edge of her nightie to reveal her scabby knees. 'Tennis is a blood sport.'

'You're meant to stay on your feet, not crawl after the ball.' His chuckle was deep and rumbly and did funny things to her insides, alternately tightening and softening her muscles. His gaze seemed fixed on her kneecaps, and the tip of his tongue appeared at the left corner of his mouth.

Tugging her nightie as far down her legs as possible, she studied him right back. Cody sitting on her couch was different to Cody attending an old man with a broken leg. She liked this version.

She liked the professional one too.

So what? She liked George at work and when he was hanging out with Jason. She enjoyed Karin in the department and when they sometimes had a meal in town on a Friday night.

But Cody? She liked...

'I'm going back to bed.' Pushing up to her feet, she swayed back and forth until the stars behind her eyeballs blinked off.

A hand took her upper arm gently. 'Take it easy.'

Pulling free of those fingers that felt like heat pads on her skin, she stumbled out of the room and down to her bedroom. Dropping onto the bed, she managed to swallow some pills and pour water down her throat— and down her chin and over the front of her nightie— before lying down and tugging the sheet over her head.

Playing ostrich in case her nurse decided to come and check on her.

'You all right under there?' Yes, the nurse had followed her. Or was that Cody the man?

Flicking the sheet off her face, she grimaced at him. It didn't work. He still leant in the doorway watching her, nothing but genuine concern in his expression. For her? No one else here, so it had to be. 'I had a dream.'

That gorgeous mouth flattened. 'A dream or a nightmare?'

'More like a movie where I had the lead role. You were in it, being as calm and useful as you were in the real deal, as was Strong—not being calm and helpful.' She licked her lips nervously. She didn't want to fall asleep and go through that again.

'At least I didn't change roles.' Cody moved, sat on the end of the bed and gave her another soft smile. She was getting to like those. 'Want a cup of tea? It might help you go to sleep. I'd tell you a story but I'm all out of them at the moment.'

Her mouth curved up in response to his smile. How could it not? Cody had a way about him that slipped through all her determination to remain aloof. A light, friendly way that did things to her insides, things that she'd thought long dead, things that weren't about friendship but about something more intense. *Not going to happen. It can't. He's bound to want children some day.* 'Tea would be lovely.'

Tea would be lovely, her brain mimicked.

What was it about this man that had her melting with just a glance? Could it be that strength of character she'd seen in play today? He hadn't faltered from the moment the so-called detective had stepped into Resus. *Be real. You were ogling him and salivating over his bod before the department's unwelcome visitor turned up.*

Whatever. Whichever way she looked at Cody, and not only at his physical attributes, he came up trumps. Fine. *Whatever*, she repeated under her breath. The fact remained she had failed at one marriage and the reasons behind that hadn't changed. She still couldn't have children, and her long hours at work hadn't lessened, not even when she'd changed jobs.

'Tea for the lady.' Cody spoke softly from somewhere above her.

Her eyes sprang open. That was quick. 'You move quietly.' But then she already knew how light he was on his feet. This morning's assailant hadn't seen him coming—at least, not as swiftly as he'd been taken down.

'If you were asleep, I didn't want to wake you.'

He only got better and better. Which was bad, bad, bad.

Cody rubbed it in some more. 'I'll listen out for you during the night in case you have another rerun of that movie.'

Her heart thudded against her ribs, while her stomach slowly melted into a pool of longing. Longing for a man who might really, really be as big-hearted and understanding of her as Cody appeared to be. *Stop these stupid dreams.* They were never for real and only came back to bite people on the backside. Hers especially.

'Thanks,' she muttered and sipped her tea. What else could she say?

It was still Friday. There were two days before she went back to work and needed to have put Cody into the slot he was meant to be in. Ah, but hadn't she kind of intimated he should go with her to Jason's birthday bash? Not with her, exactly, but she hadn't told him to stay away.

All this went to show that when a mad man put a gun to her head she couldn't be responsible for anything she did or said for some time afterwards.

Harper sank down into her pillows, pushed Cody away out of her thoughts and finished her tea, thinking about her family, all her nieces and nephews, and how much she adored them. Despite her day, she felt safe. Nothing to do with Cody. Nothing at all.

The next time she woke, daylight was lightening the edges of her not-so-good blackout curtains. Lifting her head slowly, she was relieved to find the pressure band around her skull had gone and the drummers behind her eyeballs had packed their bags and left. Yeah. Progress. She still felt wiped out and would take any movement slowly. Swallowing hurt like stink but the swelling at the front of her neck felt as though it might have lessened.

Climbing out of bed, she shoved into a tee-shirt and tugged on a pair of long gym pants—not a fashion statement, but at least she could saunter out to her kitchen and face up to Nurse Cody without blushing about her night attire.

His eyes widened and those full lips twitched when he saw her. 'You're not going to tennis, then?'

Okay, maybe a light blush. 'Has he phoned again?' Her head might be a load better but thumping around a court swinging a racket would not be the best idea she could have. It wasn't even on a good day, when all her faculties were in top working order.

'No. It's only a little after eight. Just thought that might be why you're up early. As in, early for someone who had the migraine from hell and had dealt with a mad man on her watch in the ED.'

'Eight is late for any morning of the week, no matter what's been going on.' She grinned. She couldn't help it. Cody did that to her, made her want to smile, grin, shout from the rooftop. Shout what? Um… No idea, but it probably wouldn't make a lot of sense.

'Want some breakfast? I popped out to the supermarket early on.'

The mouth-watering smell of bacon cooking tempted her. A lot. But she knew better than to give into temptation. 'Dry toast and herbal tea will do for now.' Though that bacon did smell delicious.

'No fatty food after a migraine?'

'I avoid it for a while.' Did he have to look so comfortable at the stove too? Where didn't he fit in? Her ultra-modern kitchen had never looked so good, although a bit cramped for space. He could have been on the poster for the kitchen company; they wouldn't have been able to keep up with orders.

'So, no tennis today. But you've got that birthday party and a game of cricket tomorrow.'

'My cricket skills are no better than my tennis ones. I usually keep the score.' A sportswoman she was not. But there had to be something out there she could get into and enjoy, some hobby or game that would keep her busy and her brain engaged when she wasn't working, or looking after one or other of 'the brat pack', as she called her brothers' broods. Glancing across at her dining table, she shrugged. The patchwork quilt she'd promised her mother hadn't progressed past the first few blocks.

'Nor are my sewing attempts. Though I can sew two pieces of fabric together, I get bored too soon. I must have the attention span of a gnat because the thought of making something Mum would be proud to have on her bed does my head in.'

Cody's gaze followed the direction she was staring in. 'I can't quite see you at a sewing machine. Seems too...'

'Dull? Simple?' She gave him a quick smile. 'Or complicated?'

He laughed, retrieved the pan off the hob, tipped the bacon onto a slice of toast, added pepper and slapped a second slice on top. 'You can stitch up people. I trust you to stitch fabric. Just didn't seem like your kind of hobby for some reason.'

'You might be right about that. Did you make it to the bedroom for a sleep last night, or stay on the couch?'

'I gave one of the beds a go. I slept on top. I've tidied up so the kids won't know I've even been in there.'

'To be honest they won't care who's been using their room.' Digging in the pantry, she found a packet of tea bags and a mug. 'As long as there's ice-cream in the freezer and chocolate in the cupboard, they're happy.'

'How many children have you got?'

The children question. It got to her every time even when she was used to it. Cody wasn't to know her history, so it was an innocuous question, or would be for most women.

'I haven't got any.' For a brief while there she'd felt totally at ease with this man in her apartment and forgotten the usual reasons why she didn't spend time with men who intrigued her. Now, though disappointment flared, she should be grateful to Cody once again—this time for reminding her that she was destined to remain single. Men wanted families as much as she did.

'Got that wrong, didn't I? Gemma mentioned kids yesterday, and that spare bedroom isn't decorated for any adults I've ever met.' He smiled softly.

And melted her heart just a weeny bit. 'Gemma was referring to my seven nieces and nephews, known as "the brat pack". There aren't many weekends I don't have some of them staying with me. This weekend is an exception, but then I'm going to be in Lowry Bay with them tomorrow. I might even head over tonight.'

'Seven, eh? That explains the people-mover Gemma was driving. How many of those seven are hers?'

'I'd say three. She'd say she's got four. She counts my brother as a big kid. She's right. He is.' When it came to sick or distressed children at the ED, she'd noticed Cody was a bit like Jason, with how he cheered them up by having fun. He too acted like a big kid at times. Except Cody appeared far more tidy and organised.

'Are you okay if I head away once I've cleaned up my cooking mess?' The subject of her and children was obviously done and dusted and she hadn't had to explain herself.

'I'll give you a ride to the hospital so you can collect your motorbike.' She was past the blackout phase and felt almost as good as new. Almost. A quiet day mucking about around here would do the trick. She gave another glance at her table. If she tackled that pile of fabric triangles she might bore herself into a stupor and forget Cody and migraines and assailants. Forget why she was alone and desperate to find something to occupy herself with so she didn't think about finding a man who'd love her regardless of her flaws.

CHAPTER FOUR

'HAPPY BIRTHDAY, BIG BROTHER.' Harper stretched onto her toes and kissed Jason's cheek, then handed him an envelope.

'What's this? Tickets to the one-day cricket match at the Cake Tin?' Jason was referring to the sports arena in central Wellington, so named for its resemblance to said tin.

'In your dreams, buster.' She knew their brother Noah was giving him tickets for that game. 'I've booked you into a spa for a leg wax and facial.'

'She's so funny this morning. That headache must've vamoosed completely.' He tore the envelope open with all the finesse of a one-year-old. As he read the voucher, his eyes widened with delight. 'Hey, Gemma, look at this. We're getting a break from our brats. A weekend for two in Blenheim for the wine festival. And guess who's brat-sitting?'

Harper poured herself a coffee from the pot bubbling on the gas ring and eyed up the crumpets on the bench. Not only had her head cleared but her throat had settled back to near normal and her stomach was ravenous. Spending last night here with her family had been just the cure she'd needed. She and Jason had talked about the incident in the ED which, along with knowing Cody would be there as well, helped her feel she could go back to work tomorrow morning without any qualms about the patients.

Last night Cody had texted to ask how she was. A simple message that had made her inordinately happy. But he hadn't said any more about if he'd come to the party today. He'd been reticent right from when Gemma had invited him, and she should be grateful, but that annoying devilish side to her nature was hoping he'd turn up.

'What time are we cranking up this shindig?' she asked Jason.

'First ball will be bowled at one-thirty, straight after lunch,' he replied.

'Your mum and dad will be here for lunch,' Gemma said.

'So any time soon,' Harper guessed. It was barely gone eight but no one in the White family stuck to times. They just arrived when they were ready, usually early, and everyone helped out with the food and the games and whatever else needed doing.

'I told Cody to be here in time for the cricket,' Gemma added with a wink.

Harper's mood wavered, hope warring with apprehension. Having Cody in the midst of her family was a little too close for comfort. They weren't best friends, or lovers, or anything other than work colleagues who'd been through a bit of drama together. But he did make her feel different, alive in a way she hadn't been for years. 'I have no idea what he'll do,' she admitted. In reality, Cody probably wasn't interested in attending her family celebrations. Why would he be?

'We need another fielder for the cricket.' Gemma grinned and dropped two crumpets into the toaster.

'While *you* need a big breakfast. You've hardly eaten a thing for two days.'

Darn, but the woman was bossy. Well, she wasn't getting the last word. 'I could do with losing some weight. The shorts I tried on the other day looked hideous.'

Jason laughed. 'The shorts or you in them?'

Brothers could be right pains in the backside. Harper swiped at Jason's forearm. 'Haven't you got a barbecue to haul out and clean?'

'The kids are doing that.' But he headed off to supervise, whistling tunelessly as he went.

By one o'clock all her family was sitting around the enormous outdoor table munching on sandwiches and the savouries Gemma had had everyone who'd dared step into the kitchen make. The sun was high in the clear blue sky, the temperature rising by the minute.

'It will be too hot to play cricket soon,' Harper commented.

'Never too hot,' one of the boys shouted.

'Sunscreen all round, brats.' Noah stood up and began stacking empty plates.

The roar of a motorbike blasted through the hot air, sending prickles of apprehension up Harper's spine. Cody had a motorbike.

The sound got closer, then a large bike turned into the drive. Moments later comparative silence settled. The kids raced across the lawn to gape at the fascinating machine. Harper stared at the rider pulling his helmet off. It seemed Cody Brand wasn't averse to joining her family after all.

Harper didn't know how to feel about this development. She hadn't prepared for it. She wasn't ready for the man now swinging a leg over the bike to join her family. Black leather suited him perfectly. Her heart fluttered roughly against her ribs. *Settle, girl. Settle.*

Cody looked around, locked eyes with her and nodded, a cheeky grin on his face.

Harper headed in his direction. Even if it turned out she didn't want him here, she wouldn't be rude enough to ignore him. 'Hey, this is a surprise.'

His grin didn't falter. 'You figured I'd be a no-show, huh?'

I hoped you would be. And I hoped you wouldn't. 'I forgot to factor in Gemma's powers of persuasion. No one ignores her.'

'I won't hang around for long, Harper. But as I was going past I thought I should at least stop by and say hello.'

No one went past Lowry Bay. Not unless they had something to do in Eastbourne, and she doubted Cody did. 'If you think you're…'

The rest of what she had to say was lost in shouts of glee from the children, gazing at the motorbike with excitement in their eyes.

'Wow. Does it go fast?'

'Can I have a ride?'

'I want a motorbike when I get bigger.'

Cody looked bemused for a moment, then he laughed. 'Yes, it goes fast. I'm Cody, Auntie Harper's friend.' Really? Yeah, maybe he was. 'Who are all of you?'

The eldest boy rushed in with, 'I'm Levi, he's Timothy, she's Mosey and that's Nosey.'

'Levi,' Harper warned. 'Alice and Greer,' she told Cody.

'And I'm Jason, one of Harper's brothers.' Jason held his hand out. 'Glad you dropped by. We owe you a beer or three for what you did on Friday.' The men shook hands before Jason said, 'Come and meet the rest of the clan. Hope you can bowl a straight line. Cricket starts shortly. We're just waiting for a couple of kids from down the road to turn up.'

Cody shrugged out of his heavy jacket.

Harper had to stop from reaching over and rubbing that leather. It would be warm from his body, soft where it had clung to his muscles. *Oh, for goodness' sake, stop it.* Maybe she needed a night with a gigolo. A laugh spluttered over her lips. *Yeah, right. Way to go, Harper.*

Cody glanced at her before telling Jason, 'I'm only stopping for a few minutes.'

Gemma might've been standing over on the deck but she had big ears. 'You're here now. There's no getting away from us until after dinner.'

Cody grinned and flicked his hand to his forehead. 'Yes, mam. Thank you, mam.' Then he turned to Harper, and the grin faded. 'How's that head? The migraine gone?'

'Completely. The throat's not so raw any more either. How about you? No after-effects from dropping on that man?' Did his hip need checking over? She *was* a doctor.

'It must be fine. I mowed lawns and cleaned guttering yesterday.' There was a twinkle in his eyes, as though challenging her to ask more.

Did he want her to know about his life outside the department? 'Your place? Or someone else's?' Harper picked his jacket up off the bike seat. 'Don't leave this in the direct sun.' Any excuse to hold it against her chest and breathe in the maleness of its wearer.

'Mine. I bought a house when I got to town. It's a bit of a doer-upper. Not had a lot of TLC for years, I'd say.'

'A project, then.' He hadn't said where it was, and she wasn't asking, even when she wanted to know.

'I'm not much into sports either, except when it comes to playing with kids.' He shifted his gaze from her to scan the lawn where the guys had put in wickets and mowed a pitch. 'Looks like your family is really into it. How did you miss those genes?'

'You'll have to ask my parents.'

'They're here too?' Suddenly he looked very uncomfortable. 'There are a lot of you. Maybe I shouldn't have dropped in.'

'Hey, no one bites. Come and meet everyone, get it out of the way. Kids, leave that bike alone,' she told two of the boys. 'You don't want to be knocking it off its stand and getting hurt.'

'There are two helmets,' one of them noted. 'Does that mean we can have a ride?'

Cody grimaced. 'I thought Auntie Harper might go for one with me.' As an aside, he said, 'I didn't think about the kids when I brought it with me.'

Jason called across the lawn. 'Game's starting. Cody, you need to shed some clothes, man. It's too hot to be running after a ball in leathers.'

'I've got shorts and a tee. Where can I change?' he asked Harper.

Right here would work for her. 'I'll take you inside.'

'Come with me.' Levi grabbed his hand and began hauling him across to the shed. 'Only girls get changed in the house.'

'Glad to know I'm not girlie.' Cody raised his eyebrows at her.

'Levi's aiming for a ride on that bike,' she retorted with a smile. Definitely not girlie; no way. Not with those muscles, flat abs and that unquestionably male silhouette. Jerking her head around, she pulled her gaze away from him. Phew, it was getting hotter by the second around here.

'Here, you look like you could do with something cold.' Gemma handed her a glass beaded with condensation. 'Thought water was appropriate, given that you're already half tipsy just watching Cody.'

'Get away.' She snatched the glass and gulped half the contents down.

On her other side Megan, her other sister-in-law, waved a full wine glass at the man who had everyone's attention. 'He is rather yummy.'

'Quite different to Harper's last man. Think I prefer this one,' Gemma announced.

Harper scowled. 'Haven't you two got anything better to do?'

'What could be better than winding you up?' Megan grinned. 'If you couldn't care less, then nor would we.'

'Huh.' Harper couldn't think of anything to say to shut the two up and not get more stupid comments.

'Let's get comfortable under the trees and watch how he is with a ball and bat.' Megan grabbed her arm and dragged her over to where the kids had set up the outdoor chairs.

Without thinking, Harper said, 'If he hits the ball a neighbour will be complaining about a broken window. Those are serious muscles in his arms and shoulders.'

'Knew she'd noticed,' Gemma quipped. 'You should've seen her all snuggled up to the man's chest on Friday when he carried her into her apartment. Cute as, I'm telling you. He's yet to strip down to shorts and tee.'

'Hottie' didn't begin to describe the man. 'Stop it,' she spluttered. 'I'm telling you, I am not interested.'

'That's a shame, because I've invited him to Levi's birthday party in a couple of weeks.'

'You what?' Harper spun around in her seat so fast she flipped out onto the grass.

Amidst lots of laughter from her sisters-in-law, she was hauled to her feet and pushed back into the chair. 'Oh, boy, have you got it bad or what?'

'I have not got it any damned way. You're out of order inviting Cody again. Don't ever try pushing me into a relationship. You know the score.' Anger was replacing her lighter mood, the girls' idea of fun no longer remotely enjoyable.

Megan reached over with a hug. 'Just want you to be happy, Harper. You know we don't mean much by our teasing.'

She bit down on a sharp retort. She loved these girls as much as her own sister, Suzanne, but there were times she could happily bang their heads together. 'I am happy. A lot happier than when I was married. Okay?'

'Can't argue with that. Ready for a wine?'

'Not today. Want to be on my game at work tomorrow. Oh...' Harper's eyes fixed on those hands reaching up for a ball one of the kids had hit into the air as Cody strode onto the lawn. Big hands, strong, and yet she knew how gentle they could be... They snatched the ball out of the air.

Beside her the girls went into shrieks of laughter, but at least they refrained from making any more flippant comments. Suzanne joined them and pressed a glass of low-alcohol wine into her hand. 'You'll be fine with that.'

Then Cody glanced over and she felt her insides melt, or what was left of them after the previous meltdown. One look and she was gone. How would she manage to stay sane and sensible at work when he would be around all the time? She might have to talk to George about transferring to night shift. Except she preferred days; she hated the disruption to sleep patterns that working all night brought. Her contract was for days except in emergencies, and had been hard fought for, so to change it now would be a backwards step. To change it because of Cody would be dumb.

And if she did nights she wouldn't be seeing much of this rowdy lot, and that was not about to happen. Her family meant everything to her since she'd never have her own children. She wouldn't adopt or foster as a single parent. It wasn't fair on the child. When Darren had told her he'd changed his mind and did want a family, she'd reminded him he'd been agreeable to adopting a child, but somewhere along the way he'd become dead set against *that* idea. Just another of his promises he'd reneged on. What had she seen in him?

Again she found herself watching Cody. He was chasing down a ball. When he slid into the fence, the kids cheered. He clambered to his feet, a grin splitting his face. He was having fun. No one could fake that look of pure enjoyment.

He'd make a fabulous dad.

Harper's stomach lurched. No, no, no. She'd known it was wrong to have him join her family today, and yet she'd wanted him here. Now she had the proof of why he couldn't join them ever again.

'Where are you going?' Gemma asked as she stood up.

'Need my sun hat and some more sunscreen.' And to put distance between herself and that man turning her carefully organised world upside down, inside out.

Cody heaved the ball at the wickets and missed, which won him growls from the kids and applause from the women. All the women except Harper, who seemed intent on something on the grass she was crossing, going towards the house.

What was up? Moments ago she'd been yakking with her sisters and watching his every move. *Nearly every move. Don't get big-headed.*

'Catch it, Cody,' Jason yelled.

Hell, now he was day-dreaming. Not a good look, especially amongst this lot. Leaping high, he missed the ball. Again.

Levi sidled up to him. 'You said you could play.'

'Sorry, buddy. I wasn't concentrating. I'll do better from now on, okay?' He held his hand up to high-five the youngster.

The kid grinned and slapped his hand. 'You going to take some of us for a ride later?'

He should've parked around the corner and walked here. He'd known there were kids here—what boy didn't want to ride a motorbike sometimes? Not that he minded giving each one of the brat pack a short ride but there were a lot of parents, and even grandparents, who might object for safety reasons. 'We'll talk about it later.'

Of course, Levi wouldn't let him get away with that. 'As soon as the cricket's finished?'

'It might be too late. Isn't there going to be a barbecue then?'

'There'll be time. I'm first.'

Cody nudged him. 'Your turn to bat. And I haven't said I'm taking you or any of the others for a ride yet. I have to talk to your folks.'

No one objected as long as helmets were worn, trousers replaced shorts and Cody only drove them around the park at the end of the street.

'Only if I get a ride afterwards.' Jason nodded. 'I'm the birthday boy, after all.'

'You want to ride passenger or take the bike off on your own?' Cody asked, not knowing if the guy knew how to ride.

'I'll leave you in control, and promise not to hug you too tight,' he smirked. Then he turned to the women. 'Any of you want a turn too? Gemma?'

'Of course I do.'

Cody groaned. That barbecue was going to be hours away at this rate. 'We'd better get started.'

His new friend, Levi, called, 'Grandma, do you want a turn?'

'An enormous motorbike and a good-looking man going begging? Of course I do.'

Harper chuckled beside him. 'Relax, Cody. She hates sitting in a car when anyone else is driving. You're safe.'

Everyone laughed, and Cody shook his head. Then made a mistake. 'You going to give it a whirl, Harper?'

She was going to say no. He could see it in the set of her mouth, the slightly darker gleam in her eyes and the tightening of her body.

'Don't wuss out, Harper,' Jason called. 'You've always wanted to be a biker's girl.'

Annoyance flared on that beautiful face, but she locked her eyes with his and nodded. 'Take me to Eastbourne and back.'

'I'll do better than that.' *Shut up, Cody.* 'I'll take you home at the end of the day.'

'I've got my car here.' She was looking stunned that she'd even agreed to go in the first place.

'I'll drop it off at the hospital tomorrow when I go for my scan,' Suzanne said.

'Scan?' Shock froze on Harper's face. Around them, everyone else was yelling and jumping up and down.

'You're pregnant? Yippee' was the general chorus.

'We were going to tell you all next weekend, since this is Jason's birthday, but it sort of slipped out.' A pink-faced Suzanne leaned into the man who'd just draped his arm over her shoulders. 'We've been waiting until the first twelve weeks were up before saying a word. It's been so hard to keep quiet.'

'Especially for you.' Noah was the first to give his sister a hug and shake his brother-in-law's hand.

Harper still appeared shell-shocked. Didn't she want any more nieces and nephews? No, Cody decided, there was more to her reaction than that. That'd be petty and, as far as he'd seen, Harper didn't do petty. He moved closer to her, not touching, but there for her.

Jason was watching Harper and nodded when he saw what Cody had done.

So what was her problem? When Harper took her turn to hug her sister, she struggled to let go and seemed to hold tighter, harder, longer than anyone else. Did she want a baby too? Was she jealous of her sister—when she didn't have a man in her life? But then he didn't know if there was or wasn't a partner somewhere. Just because she'd come alone to her brother's party didn't mean there wasn't a man out there who was Harper's other half. A very absent other half. Except she seemed taken with *him* at times. Now he was really confused.

'It's going to be fine.' Suzanne rubbed Harper's back and looked helplessly over her shoulder to her brothers.

Jason grabbed Noah as he made to take Harper's arm. 'Let's get the kids back playing cricket for a bit longer. Harper's going for a ride on that Harley.'

Cody got the message loud and clear, even if Harper

hadn't. When he turned her towards his bike she hesitated and glanced up at him, and then across to her brother.

Jason nodded once. 'Go blow some cobwebs out of your head, sis, and then Cody can be driven crazy by giving all these kids a short spin around the park.'

Suzanne caught Harper's hand. 'Go on, get out of here for a bit. I'm sorry how I blurted it out, but it's been hard holding it back. It's so exciting, and—' She bit off whatever else she'd been going to say.

Harper wrapped her arms around her sister. 'Don't you dare be sorry. It's wonderful news. Really and truly. I'm happy for you both.'

Cody brought the spare helmet across and handed it to her. When she quickly placed it on her head and began fumbling with the straps, he knew she was desperate to get away for a while. 'Let me.' He took the straps and did them up tight enough to keep the helmet in place, but not so tight that her skin was scrunched, or made that still-tender throat uncomfortable. Her warm, soft skin was velvet against his fingers.

'Put these on.' Gemma handed over a jacket and some track pants to Harper. 'You'll freeze otherwise.'

'Where shall we go?' she asked quietly, her mind obviously still absorbing her sister's news.

'Wait and see.' He shucked into his jacket, hauled his leather trousers over his shorts, then straddled the bike and waited for her to climb up behind him, before roaring the engine into life.

'Hold on tight,' he said over his shoulder, and then drew a sharp breath when she wound her arms around him and laid her face against his back. He'd taken many people for rides on his bike over the years, quite a few of them women, but not once had he experienced the heat and longing from a pair of arms around his upper body and a face lying tucked in against him as was pouring through him this minute. He mightn't want Harper White to be anyone special, but he sure as hell seemed to be having trouble keeping her on the same uninvolved level as any other woman he'd known since Sadie.

This was going to be a long ride, even if he only took her to the end of the road—all of three hundred metres. Suddenly he was afraid. Afraid that Harper was sneaking in under his radar, touching him in ways he'd never thought to know again. That couldn't happen.

'We going today?' The sharp question came near his ear and had him revving the engine louder and faster than he'd normally do.

'Sure thing, doctor,' he muttered, knowing she'd never hear him over the bike noise.

He took her through the township of Eastbourne and on toward Pencarrow Head, until they were alone apart from the seagulls and the wild shoreline, and then stopped the bike. 'Let's stroll along the water's edge,' he suggested as the roar of the engine died. He needed a break from those arms still encircling him before he did something they'd both regret. Kissing came to mind. Along with touching.

'I'd like that.'

She was talking about the walk, right? He turned on the seat and stared at her, sure his thoughts were easy to read and still unable to look away.

Harper sprang off the bike fast, as though she also wanted space between them. 'Do I leave the helmet with the bike? Or would it be best to carry it in case someone comes along?'

Cody shook his head. 'I doubt anyone with bad intentions will turn up in the next half hour.'

She slipped the helmet onto the handle bar. 'You can say that even after what happened on Friday? We never saw Strong coming.'

Of course she was still shaken by that. It'd have been more surprising if she wasn't. 'I'll take a chance on our helmets being here when we get back.'

Harper clambered over rocks to reach the sand, the breeze lifting her hair behind her. Long, shiny hair that made him ache to finger-comb it, made his manhood throb with need.

Damn it, he should never have visited the White family in the first place. Should've gone to visit his mother instead. But he'd taken his mother out to lunch yesterday and had learned she was unwell with a summer cold. The rest-home nurses thought she'd be better tucked up in bed today without visitors. He'd wanted to argue but had given in to the idea of joining Harper's family for the afternoon.

He ambled along behind Harper, drinking in the sight of her firm legs and gently swaying buttocks, wishing he'd followed through on that urge to kiss her, no matter the consequences.

He caught up with her when she paused to watch the inter-island ferry make its way between Pencarrow and Palmer Heads on its way to the South Island.

'I can't have children.' She continued staring across the water to the boat. 'But you probably already figured that out.'

He took her hand and began walking farther along the stony beach. 'No, I hadn't got to that answer yet.' He'd deliberately stopped thinking about her reaction to her sister's news the moment Jason had suggested he take her for a ride. He hadn't wanted to dwell on what he doubted he'd learn the answer to—not today, anyway. Who'd have thought Harper would just out and tell him? 'I can see why your sister's news upset you.'

'It shouldn't. I've had loads of experience of dealing with being told one of my family's having a baby, so I know how not to react.' Her fingers tightened around his as she spoke, and Cody wondered if she even realised they were holding hands.

He should let go. He'd only taken her hand as a comfort gesture and to move her on along the beach, yet he did not want to pull away. The warmth from her palm against his, the softness of those fingers interlaced with his, was the most wonderful sensation he'd known in a long time. So ordinary and yet so thrilling. Damn but he was turning into a softie.

Harper was still talking, as though getting something off her chest. 'I'm the godmother to every one of the brat pack.' She flicked him a quick look and he knew she hadn't finished.

But he also had something to say. 'No surprise there,' he told her before adding, 'They adore you, if what I've seen so far is anything to go by.'

'Chocolate and doing fun things will always get me that.' She smiled softly. Bending down, she picked up a handful of sand and let it dribble through her fingers as they walked, while her other hand still firmly held his. 'But being an aunt, even the best one out, doesn't take the place of raising my own children. Having my own babies.' Her sigh was so sad, Cody's heart clenched. 'I thought I had a chance to be a mum once, but the plans got changed.'

'I can't imagine what it must be like for you.' He couldn't. It was something he'd never considered, instead always believing that one day he'd have a family, teach his son to fish, or even his daughter, for that matter. But never to have his own child? Unimaginable. No wonder Harper had looked gutted when her sister had blurted out her news. No wonder Suzanne had been upset about how she'd spilled the beans. But then there'd have been no easy way to tell Harper.

'I guess no one thinks about it unless faced with the fact. I certainly didn't. Or maybe I was fooling myself, hiding from the truth. Coming from a largish family who all seem intent on doubling the world's population, the idea I couldn't contribute was implausible.'

He would've laughed at her attempt to lighten the mood but he was all out of laughs at the moment. This was something big, something that would've changed Harper's life. He had this inexplicable urge to make her feel better, but there was no way he could do that. This went deep, was very personal. It was surprising that she'd even shared it with him. What would she do if he gave her a hug? It wouldn't be quite like the hugs she got from her family. No way could he do platonic with this woman. Not any more, if he'd been able to at all. 'Can I ask why you can't have children?'

Her silence told him he'd gone too far. Fair enough. He'd known that the moment the words fell out, but she'd been so forthcoming up until now, he hadn't stopped to consider how much he could ask. Now she'd be wanting to head back to Lowry Bay and telling him to carry on to the city alone.

He resumed walking, back in the direction of his bike.

'I was born without a womb.'

Cody paused and turned slowly, so as not to make her suddenly change her mind about talking to him.

Harper sank to her haunches, scooped up more sand

and watched it dribble back to the ground. 'It wasn't picked up until my teens. I mean, why would it be?'

He dropped down beside her and took her hand again. 'Bloody hell, Harper. What were the odds, eh?' His heart was pounding at the thought of what it must've been like for her to find out.

'Higher than you'd think.' She sat down and wound her arms around her legs, resting her chin on top of her knees. 'I should remember that on days like today. I'm not the only one.'

'But as the years have gone by it's been harder to deal with?'

'Yeah, something like that.' She turned her head slightly so she could see his face.

His heart lurched at the sadness in her eyes. Hell, he'd seen almost every emotion in those beautiful eyes over the last couple of days. Even love, when she gazed at her nieces and nephews. This was one amazing woman, who gave of herself completely, even after all that had happened to her on Friday.

Without thinking, he reached for her, drew her close, wound his arms around her and lowered his mouth to hers. He kissed her slowly, as tenderly as possible, while his body was demanding, hard and hot. When she whimpered under his lips he deepened his kiss slowly. He wanted to dive right in, to taste her and hold her as close as possible, tight, but he held back, half-expecting a slap around the ears.

Until her hands began sliding up his chest to his head, her fingers pushing through his hair to massage his scalp. Then he knew this was right—for both of them. Come what may. Tomorrow they might regret it, today... Today he was living a dream, was kissing the woman who had him in turmoil all the time.

Her mouth opened under his and he slid his tongue across into her hot cavern and tasted her. His heart stuttered. Raw, hot need clawed through his gut and headed downward to where he expressed his need so effortlessly. *Easy, boy, easy.* Even in his fogged-up brain he knew acting on that impulse would be going too far. For now, he had to be happy with this sizzling kiss. And, hell, was Harper sizzling. What a woman. He melted in against her, held her tighter and kissed her until they both ran out of air.

Harper finally drew back, taking those lips just out of reach. Her breasts rose and fell too quickly. A delectable shade coloured her cheeks and her eyes were shining. 'Wow,' she whispered, running her finger over her top lip. 'Wow.'

That was one word for what had just passed between them. 'Hot' and 'intense' were two more. 'Unbelievable' would be another.

And downright disturbing.

Where did they go from here? 'Bed' was the first word to pop into his skull. But, despite everything, he still knew that wasn't happening today. There'd be repercussions, possibly insurmountable, if they stripped down naked and had their way with each other. He wanted Harper with every fibre of his body. He suspected she felt the same. But there was a wariness creeping into the stunned look in her eyes which told him to put the brakes on. His libido was going nowhere right now.

Pulling back so her eyes met his, she stared into him, deeply, right in. Looking for...? He had no idea; he only hoped he measured up to her expectations.

Then her mouth opened and the question tripped out,

low and filled with despair. 'Do you want children of your own one day?'

Now, there was a loaded question. If he said no, he'd be lying; if he said yes, whatever was unfolding between them would be gone in a flash.

He wouldn't lie. 'Yes. I do.' He pulled back and tossed a pebble down the beach to splash in the water. 'Not that it's likely to ever happen,' he added quietly.

To have a family, he'd have to risk his heart again. He'd have to believe he could protect her no matter what turned up. He wasn't ready to trust himself with someone yet.

CHAPTER FIVE

JASON SPRAWLED OVER the chair beside Harper, stretched out his legs in front, scratched his chest and yawned.

'Very attractive,' Harper drawled. 'No wonder Gemma calls you one of the brat pack.'

'She loves me as I am.' His mouth softened into a gentle smile as his eyes searched out his wife amongst all the kids hanging around the barbecue, where Cody was doing as he was told and cooking a mound of sausages and chops. Between Gemma and the kids, their new friend wasn't getting any free time to do as he pleased.

Harper pressed her lips—her well-kissed and still tender lips—together. Thank goodness. Somehow Cody voicing what had been no surprise about wanting a family was hard to swallow. There was no reason why she should care one way or the other, but his simple, 'Yes,' had provoked a tide of longing and sadness to overwhelm her. Coming after that bone-melting, knee-shaking kiss, she'd been lost, completely unable to compute everything and make sense of it all.

That kiss had blitzed her brain. Being held in those strong arms had given her a sense of belonging she didn't think she'd ever known before. She'd loved Darren with all her being, or so she'd thought. But not one kiss with him had given her the deep yearning for more that Cody's had. Or was that just because enough time had passed to forget things she and Darren had shared? But Cody's kiss had been unbelievable. Shattering. Life-changing. If she let it be. Which she couldn't. In the end, everything came back to her inability to have children. Even if Cody accepted that and went with whatever was unfolding between them she knew even the sincerest of promises could, and most likely would, be broken. She wasn't up to withstanding that a second time. Hell, she couldn't ask a man to give up his dreams for her. Not again. She'd learned it was too much to ask of any one.

There was no denying Cody's honesty. He must've known it would hurt her, and yet he'd still gone with the truth. She admired him for that. But in the end she'd demanded to be brought back here in the hope that being surrounded by her family could put some perspective on what had really only been a kiss. One hell of a kiss. It'd been hard not to ask him to drop her off and head away so she didn't have to see him and confront what was really getting her knickers in a knot—the fact she was becoming increasingly attracted to him. Unfortunately, the kids had had other ideas, namely their promised rides on the back of his motorbike, and he was still here after obliging them.

'He's got you in a right old twist,' Jason drawled.

Harper slapped her head. They'd been talking about Gemma. Nothing to do with Cody. Yet her very astute brother knew where she'd gone in her mind. To bring things back on track, and away from what felt like dangerous ground, she said, 'Gemma needs her head read, the way she puts up with you despite all your bad habits.'

What was it like to feel so safe with another person's love that you could act completely naturally all the time? To feel safe enough to be able to relax about everything? She'd thought she had that with Darren until he'd dropped his verbal grenade. Apparently he hadn't loved her more than anything or anyone, or enough to accept they wouldn't have children. He had accepted that. Only not in the way she'd believed. *They* wouldn't have children, but he would—with another woman.

One day as she'd strolled along Auckland's Mission Bay, trying yet again to make up her mind about what to do with her life now that she was separated from her husband, Harper had seen the dark-haired woman he'd left her for sitting and drinking coffee with girlfriends. At least, she'd presumed it was coffee. What she'd been absolutely certain about was the very mature baby bump that had said clearer than words that Darren had been with this woman before he'd left his wife. That scene had torn her apart, underscored the truth—there would be no reconciliation, no matter that she might forgive him if he came begging.

It had also added a final layer of protection around her heart. She would never, ever, put her heart on the line again. It would be her own fault if she fell for a man and then had to go through another break-up. She'd finally come to accept she had no right ask a man to give up his dreams of having a family.

'He's an all-right guy.' When Jason spoke so casually, he was usually hiding something.

He had a name. 'Define "all right".'

'I don't think I need to. You seem taken with him.'

Harper studied the man who'd been bugging the hell out of her head all weekend. Good-looking: tick. Kind: tick. Great with kids: tick. So what? Sexy, intriguing and annoying with his confidence: tick, tick, tick. 'I work with him. I like him. He was incredible in ED on Friday, so calm and constantly alert to the possibility of taking the creep down. Do I want to get to know him better?' *Yes. No.* 'I don't know.' She answered her own question honestly. 'But I do know I'm not going to.'

Just then Cody looked across the lawn directly at her and winked. Her mouth tipped up into a big smile. Warmth filled her. Yeah, she could get used to a man like Cody. And those kisses. But she wasn't going to, she repeated to herself. He wanted children.

'Sis, stop beating yourself up. It's wearing for you, and for all of us. Life threw you a hard ball, but we all get those.'

She gasped. Jason never talked to her like this. He was the fun brother, the easy sop who loved everyone and didn't want to stir up emotions. 'Says the man with three boys to adore.'

'You have seven nieces and nephews who love you as much as their parents and who spend a lot of time with you. You don't get the sleepless nights, or the arguments about what's for dinner, just the fun times. Yes, there's another on the way. Suzanne and Steve are ecstatic. You can't avoid that and, face it, you won't want to.'

Another black mark to erase. She didn't used to be so selfish, had always been thrilled every time one of her sisters-in-law had announced they were pregnant. But Suzanne's words had thrown her. Her baby sister was joining the parent club and she'd felt more left out than ever. 'I reacted badly.'

'You did.' Jason sipped his beer. 'Be grateful for what you've got and stop dwelling on what you can't have.'

'Easy for you to say,' she snapped as guilt and disappointment warred in her head. She hated that Jason thought her ungrateful, but he should try a little harder to understand.

'Remember that career I always wanted as a lawyer with our foreign service?' he said suddenly.

'The one you were determined to get even when you were still in nappies?'

'Yes, that one. I was offered a position with Foreign Affairs last year.' He stared across the lawn at his wife and children. 'I turned it down because my family mean too much to me. I couldn't bear to take them out of their home and schools and away from their friends for the sake of my own desires.'

'They'd have a wonderful life living in different countries.'

'They'd have had to make new friends every few years as we moved from country to country, probably have to go to boarding school for high-school education. I couldn't do that to Gemma. I couldn't live without my kids with me either.'

Harper looked sideways at her brother. 'You never told me.'

'You were working your butt off in Auckland, trying to get beyond Darren and his broken promises, trying to decide what to do next. You didn't need my disappointment as well.'

'But I'm your sister. We share everything.' But guilt came fast. She had been withdrawn and selfish during that time. Who knew what she might've said to Jason if she'd known what he'd been going through? Harper laid her hand over his. 'I'm sorry. I know how much you've always wanted a career with Foreign Affairs.' She sat quietly for a few minutes, absorbing this new information. 'How did Gemma feel about you taking the job?'

'She backed me either way—said it was important that I was happy. She was more than content to pack up house and shift to Toronto, our first posting, if that's what I wanted. But I knew it wasn't what she wanted, that she was afraid to move away from where she felt safe.'

Gemma had grown up in a welfare home. Her family and home were the most important things in her life—had made her feel grounded for the first time ever. Yet she was big-hearted enough to go anywhere with Jason no matter what the cost to her.

Harper sighed. 'You're a lucky man, Jason White. I understand you've missed your opportunity in a career you always dreamed about, but you've got a wonderful wife and family, and your current position as head legal advisor to the fishing industry is nothing to be sneezed at.' She was very proud of him. As she was of Noah and Suzanne.

'Exactly. I've lost one dream, but I've got so much more. As you have, if only you'd let go of the impossible dream and see what you've already got. Stop trying to change what you can't, and get on with finding the life you want, sis.' Jason stood up and looked down at her. 'You're smitten with Cody. We can all see it. Do something about it. Don't waste an opportunity for happiness.'

Harper stared at him as he headed towards the cheerful gathering around the barbecue. What did he know? That bit about not getting everything you wanted was all very well, but wanting a family was inherent in her. Growing up with loving parents who'd also doted on each other had taught her how important a strong, trusting relationship was. Not to mention having brothers and a sister, one of whom she could happily beat around the head right now. Jason didn't know what he was talking about.

And now her headache was back, banging inside her

skull, adding to her annoyance with the world. With her brother. With Cody.

But she had an apology to make. Where had Suzanne got to?

'Right, who's next?' At the ED counter Harper picked up the top patient file. Monday mornings weren't usually as frantic as this one had turned out to be. Probably a good thing, as it kept her mind off gun-toting strangers. And Hottie in scrubs. Scrubs would never be as bland and boring again. Cody certainly filled his out a treat. Flapping the file in front of her face, she tried not to grin when Karin laughed. 'It would be rude not to notice.'

'What did I tell you?'

'What's next?' the man himself asked as he approached the counter, moving those muscles like a panther. No wasted movement, all stealth and strength.

Patients. That was why she was here. Not because of a sexy man. *More's the pity.* A quick scan told her, 'A toddler with a button up his nose.'

Cody gave her a guarded smile. 'Small children and orifices—not always a good look.'

How had she got partnered with Cody today of all days? She'd tossed and turned most of the night because of him invading her brain matter, reliving that kiss so often she thought she could be ruined for any other man and his kisses. She might as well join the nunnery now. Spending the day working alongside him would only add to the tension tightening her own muscles, turning her stomach into a washing machine on spin.

She needed to be distant with him. How did she do that when she knew what it felt like to have those arms wound around her? And those lips on hers? But… Always a but. They wanted different— No, they hoped to obtain similar things out of life. But those things could never match up between them. So to avoid heartache she was determined to remain totally professional around him. Starting now. A couple of hours late, but at least she could begin as she meant to go on.

Except it was as though everyone else thought they should be together after what they'd shared here on Friday. The talk going around the department was still about the body packer and his boss, but at least no one was asking endless questions about how she or Cody felt any more. While meant kindly, those questions had become tiring, and had hindered her determination to put it all behind her. It hadn't been as easy as she'd thought to come to work today. She'd had to deliberately toughen her stance and put on a neutral face, but every time she walked past Resus One a cold shiver slid down her spine and she found herself looking over her shoulder, fully expecting to find a gun in her face.

She'd thought she was hiding it well until Cody had said quietly, 'Resus One's never going to be the same, is it?'

She'd looked at him, ready to snap that she was fine, but had met only empathy in those vivid green eyes. *Of course.* 'Not for a while, any rate.'

Those eyes, if not that voice, would be the undoing of all her good intentions. *Face it, Harper, those intentions are already unravelling.* She straightened her already straight back. She could lock gazes with the man and not feel her knees knock. Couldn't she? Better not try to find out now. There were patients waiting. Was it possible to fall in lust this quickly? *Quickly?* It had been over a week since Cody had started working here, days since he'd been her hero in Resus One. Falling in love only took an instant in some cases.

Love? Lust. *Love?* Crazy. Not when she'd vowed to avoid that particular emotion again. That didn't count family and friends, but Cody could never be just an every day kind of friend. She'd never be able to look at him without wondering what the follow up to his kisses would be like. Oh, she had her suspicions. But that was only the physical side of things. There was plenty more to Cody than his hot bod and those divine lips. Characteristics that were equally attractive as his body.

'Harper? Hello. Where have you gone this time?' Cody still stood in front of her.

'What do you mean, this time?'

'We were talking about Resus One and you went all blank on me.'

Not blank, but at least she could be grateful he hadn't known what was going on in her head. 'Resus One. That's what we talking about.' A glance at the innocuous room still had her shivering.

Cody shrugged. 'We could hold a party in there to banish the bad vibes.'

'A fancy dress one.' And just like that she relaxed, dropping the façade of being only a colleague who knew next to nothing about him. Not what she intended at all. But she couldn't seem to help it. There was a lot of talk doing the rounds about the hug she and Cody had shared after the police had taken the gunman away. Apparently it had looked seriously intense. The people talking about it didn't know the half of it. Harper's heartbeat went double-time every time she thought about it.

He said, 'You'd come as a pirate, brandishing a sword and slaying anything that moved.'

'Actually, I do a better parrot, all feathers and squawks.'

His eyes widened. 'A parrot?'

'Yes, with a very long beak, all the better to peck kids with, and claws that hold chocolate cake.' Her smile broadened as it came from deep inside. Yeah, it was good talking with Cody like this. It was good being with Cody full stop—therein lay the problem. But right now she couldn't be bothered with problems. She was tired, hungry and so ready for a strong coffee.

'This I have to see. Whose birthday is next in the brat pack?'

'Your biggest fan.'

'Of course. How could I forget when Levi mentioned it at least ten times? But he's getting too old for parrots. Or pirates.' Cody shook his head. 'Here I was, hoping to see you with your cake claws out.'

Harper rolled her eyes with amusement. Cody had been such a hit yesterday, he'd been invited to the next birthday party in her family. It was kind of cool, really. If she hadn't been trying to avoid him. Maybe she should toughen up and go with whatever came out of this liaison. Have some fun, enjoy the moment. *Eek.* Scary. Exciting.

Loud cries came from behind the curtains of Cubicle Three, thankfully interrupting her frightening train of thought. 'That's our cue.' Pushing the curtain aside, she went to meet their small patient. 'Hello, Jarrod. I'm Harper, the doctor who's going to make you better.'

The little boy yelled louder and the man sitting on the bed holding him, presumably his dad, looked uncomfortable. 'Sorry, but he's got himself into a bit of a state.'

'Hey, Jarrod, what's this?' Cody stepped up with his hand twisted into the shape of a…?

Harper had no idea, but Jarrod stopped yelling long enough to stare at the fingers that were now wiggling at him.

'It's Bobby the Bunny. Look what he can do.' Cody made hopping gestures across the bed, pulled faces and made ridiculous noises.

And had Jarrod completely entranced.

Harper sighed. No surprise there. Yesterday she'd learned how good he was with kids. Introducing herself to the man holding Jarrod, she confirmed he was his dad. 'Has Jarrod tried blowing his nose hard?'

'Lots of times at first, but then it hurt, so he stopped.'

'Any idea how big this button is?'

'Bigger than a shirt button, but not by too much, if I've got the right one.'

Harper moved closer. 'Jarrod, can I can look up your nose? Bobby Rabbit will be here watching you, okay?'

Jarrod screamed and turned his head into his father's shoulder.

Not okay, then. 'You're going to have to hold him firmly while I take a look,' she instructed the father. 'Nurse, can you turn Jarrod's head for me?'

After a fast and awkward exam, Harper shook her head. 'That's jammed at the top. I'm going to have to sedate him so that I can pull the button out with tweezers.'

'Wait a moment.' Cody disappeared before she had time to ask where he thought he was going.

Who's the doctor around here? Her bonhomie faded. Another reason why she had to keep that distance: Cody had no right to think he could take charge.

The curtain flicked open as Cody returned. He held his hand under Jarrod's nostrils. 'Big breath through your nose, buddy.'

'Pepper?' Harper shook her head sharply. 'I don't think a sneeze is going to fix this. That button's jammed tight.'

The first two sneezes proved her right. The third

one sent the offending round of plastic flying across the floor.

'Good boy, way to go.' Cody held his palm up in front of the bemused boy. 'High five, man.'

Jarrod's hand was ridiculously tiny against Cody's, but his smile was huge. 'High five, Bobby Rabbit.'

'Thank you, Nurse Brand,' she said, quietly enough he probably didn't hear. She wasn't sure she wanted him to. Reverting to calling him Nurse Brand underlined the fact he was bringing the worst out in her. He had her reacting to his charm as though it was something to be beaten into submission. *Afraid?* a niggly little voice in the back of her head taunted. Very. But she needed to remember that not every charmer was on a mission to hurt her as Darren had. They weren't getting the chance.

'Let's take a break while we can,' Cody said. 'We're late for lunch as it is.'

'You go ahead. I'm not hungry yet.'

'So that gurgling I've been hearing for the last thirty minutes is all in my imagination?' Cody shrugged casually, but his eyes were full of disappointment. 'It's not going to be easy for you to keep your distance from me in here. Staff take breaks as they can, regardless of who they're working with.'

'I just think—' What the blazes *did* she think? Before seeing Jarrod, she'd relaxed enough to be happy around Cody; now she wanted to avoid him. *Yep. Definitely afraid. So, toughen up and deal with it, with him.* First, he was right—staff went for a break with whoever else was going, regardless of their role in the department. Even George was happy to drink coffee with a porter or junior nurse, so what was her problem? 'Let's go. Canteen or the café over the road?'

Bewilderment shoved aside that disappointment

in Cody's eyes. Shaking his head at her, he managed, 'Café,' before heading for the staff room and his locker.

All too soon she was seated at a tiny table in a cosy corner of the café with Cody's knees knocking up against hers in the cramped space. Trying to move her legs to avoid him proved awkward and made her feel stupid, so she stayed put. Enjoyed the moment. Plates of food sat on the table between them; steam rose from mugs of black coffee. She forgot to remain aloof. 'You're good with children. Jarrod would've done anything you asked.'

'Kids don't look past what you're offering, just take you at face value. It's kind of refreshing.' As he bit into his pie, small flakes of pastry dropped onto his shirt.

It would be too easy to reach across and brush them off. One sandwich did not need two hands to hold it, but how else was she to keep them out of trouble? She bit into the bread and salad, chewing thoughtfully. When she'd swallowed the tasteless lump of what had been tomato and lettuce she told Cody, 'You're a lot like my brothers. Fun, and happy to act the clown if it gets you a laugh. You'll make a great dad to those kids you want one day.'

Cody took another bite of his pie, obviously not in a hurry to carry on that conversation.

Suddenly everything he'd said on the beach yesterday came back to her. Not just the bit about him wanting a family. 'You said having a family was unlikely for you. Why? Has someone hurt you so much you won't contemplate another relationship?'

The shutters dropped over his usually friendly gaze so fast she shivered. 'Eat your lunch, doctor. We've got a busy department awaiting us.'

She'd gone too far. All because Cody was getting to

her and her only defence to that was that, by getting to know more about him, she could find reasons for not wanting to have anything else to do with him other than at work. Her sandwich suddenly seemed dry in her mouth. She'd upset him, and that was the last thing she wanted. *Should've thought before putting her mouth into gear.*

It came from being out of practice at small talk, she supposed. Having been through a lot with Cody in the last few days was no excuse. 'I'm sorry. I expect people to mind their own business when it comes to my private life, and yet I've just overstepped the mark with you. I'm truly sorry,' she repeated.

Pushing his chair back, he stood, looming over her, though she thought that was unintentional, merely an occupational hazard stemming from being so tall. 'I've forgotten what you asked already. See you back at work. I've got a prescription to pick up for my mother.'

As he threaded his way through the lunchtime crowd, his broad shoulders tight, his head high, even through her irritation Harper felt her heart lurch.

See? This was why she had to stay clear of any involvement with Cody. The risk of being hurt frightened her. She'd heard Jason's warning yesterday, knew he might even be right, but that didn't make it any easier to take that first step off the tightrope she currently walked. Along with the fact she couldn't have children, she'd lost the dream of a happy marriage, which was even more important to her. She'd put heart and soul into the one she'd had with Darren. She'd loved him completely and utterly, would've done anything for him, given him everything. Yet in the end all he'd asked of her was his freedom.

The mug of coffee shook in her hands. She needed

something big to distract her from all this so that one morning she could wake up and say, 'Yes, I am truly happy with my lot.' Something that had nothing to do with Cody Brand. Because like it or not he seemed to have taken over her mind, her feelings, her body.

Patchwork and tennis hadn't worked. What should she try next? Abseiling? She shuddered. Not likely. Time to stop trying out all these different hobbies. She didn't need a hobby. She needed to make the most of what she already had. Which was a lot. Between doctoring and family there wasn't much spare time anyway. Even if she wanted to get bored and sew together all those pieces of fabric she'd painstakingly cut up in the first place there just wasn't enough time.

Which reminded her—she needed to cancel the order for a paddle-board. As if she was going to go out in the harbour with only a board and a paddle to get around...

Cody strode down the road, intent on reaching the pharmacy and putting distance between himself and Harper so as to clear his head of her, as a woman he had the hots for, before he had to go back and work alongside her as a doctor.

He could've used the hospital dispensary to get his mother's tablets but the air in there was stifling. Nothing to do with the hot summer's day either. This might be turning out to be the hottest summer on record but his discomfort came from being close to a fiery woman with a delicious mouth and beautiful eyes. A woman who kissed like an angel. And who asked far too many questions that probed places best left alone. The risk to his heart had increased tenfold since yesterday. Huh? Try since Friday, and that monster. Time to get some control back, tighten the hatches and keep her out.

Harper. Doctor. Adored aunt. Beloved sister and sister-in-law. Fun and amusing. Sad and unhappy.

For the life of him, he didn't fully understand her sadness. Sure, there was that baby thing. He got it. Really got it. If he couldn't have a family, he'd be gutted. But he'd swear there was more going on with her. He should just ask her outright. Like she asked him things he didn't want to answer? Have her stalking off in a huff? Exasperation trickled over his lips. He'd done wrong. Shouldn't have walked away from Harper's questions. He wasn't playing fair. Not with her. He was looking out for himself.

'Ten minutes,' the pharmacist's assistant told him as she read the script.

'Fine.' He headed outside to look at paint and wallpaper in the decorating shop next door.

'Can I help you?' asked a young, over-enthusiastic woman from behind the counter.

'Just looking,' he replied and suffered a flat smile in return, which made him feel bad. 'I'm still deciding what colours I want to use inside my house.' Now, there was a joke.

'Are you going to do every room the same? Or have different shades for bedrooms and the living areas?'

The problem with playing nice was it became difficult to get away without upsetting someone. As Harper had just found out. 'Maybe one colour, with different shades of it for different areas.'

He'd really upset Harper. There'd been annoyance on her face when he'd walked away at the café, which ramped up his guilt. They'd talked about her personal life quite a lot since he'd first taken her home to her apartment on Friday. Today's conversation was only a continuation of getting to know each other better. But he didn't do talking about his life, past or present. People read too much into things.

'Here're some paint charts to take home.' The girl shoved a small bundle at him and hurried off to talk to another man coming in the door.

'Thanks,' he called as he passed her on his way out. *Hope you have better luck with him than you did with me—on all counts.*

'What are you up to?' The voice of the person he'd been avoiding caught up with him as he reached the hospital entrance. 'Are those colour charts you've got there?'

Damn. 'Thinking of painting my bedroom,' he grunted, which was true. There was also the rest of the five-bedroomed house that was in serious need of fresh paint, amongst other things.

'You've got a lot of charts for one small room.' Harper's laugh was strained.

'It's a big decision.' He managed to smile back.

'How is your sense of colour?'

Crap. 'I'm colour-blind. Like, completely colour-blind.' He swore under his breath. That opened the door—wide.

Sure enough, Harper walked right in. 'Want some input? I managed to choose the colours for my apartment without making a botch-up.'

He'd already walked away from her questions once today. He really didn't feel up to doing it again, even if it meant disclosing more about himself than he was prepared to do. He tried for tactful. 'You're too busy. Anyway, it's only a room. The colour's not a major problem.' That wasn't really true. The whole house would look a disaster if he ended up painting it bright orange or another equally appalling colour. At least, he'd assumed from other people's reaction to his previous attempts at decorating that orange was a bad choice if he wanted soft and subtle.

'Of course.' Her tone was flat.

Didn't do so well, buddy. He huffed a sigh. 'I'm sorry. I mean, thank you, Harper, I'd appreciate your help. But you have to promise me one thing.'

She turned wary eyes on him. 'Yes?'

'That you won't set me up. Pick purple or magenta just because you can get away with it.'

Merriment flooded those beautiful eyes that he hadn't been able to forget for days. 'Tell me how you even know what magenta is. Or what purple might look like on your walls.'

'I don't.' He stood absolutely still, his gaze locked on those eyes that sucked him in and made him feel like he was drowning. Silently he willed her to keep laughing. He loved the sound of her laughter, the sight of it in her face and on her mouth; in the honest way she stood in front of him. She was a sexy package, but add laughter and she became something else. Adorable. Lovable. Lovable? *Gulp. Where were they? Colours. Right.* 'But it won't take long for someone to tell me I've screwed up.'

What was he doing here? Why was he inviting her into his home? He should be doing all in his power to walk away because she'd never want to take their friendship to the next level, even if he decided to take a risk. He should even be grateful that she wouldn't. But right this moment he wanted to enjoy the glow, feel her warmth, be with her.

Her smile widened with mischief. 'I guess you'll just have to wait for the verdict, then.'

'You're having fun at my expense.' He tried growling the words but his voice only came out light and happy.

'You bet.' Then she tugged a pager from her pocket and her smile faded. 'We're on. A stat one's coming through the door.'

As they rushed to the department Harper continued giving him the brief details. 'A multiple car pile-up on the Hutt Motorway. Five patients expected in the next ten minutes.'

'All hands on deck.' That would keep him busy and make the afternoon fly by. Fingers crossed there were no fatalities, before or during the patients' time in the ED.

'When's a good time to come look at your room and those paint charts?' Harper asked as they reached the staff room. 'Tonight?'

He shook his head. 'Not tonight.' Nor tomorrow, nor any time until he decided how far he was going with this—this need building up muscle by muscle inside him. 'I'll be out.' He'd agreed she could help because he'd felt bad about walking out on her in the café, but he couldn't have her in his home. That would be getting too cosy. 'I'll let you know when I've got a free night.'

'Your social life's that busy?' Her grin was a little sick looking, making him go from feeling bad to worse.

It just seemed he couldn't get it right with this woman. 'I'm always busy, not often socially.' That was a cryptic answer, and at the screwing up of her face he decided to put her out of her misery a little. 'I visit my mother often, and tonight I'm busy catching up with old mates from when I went to school here.' One, anyway. He was having dinner with Trent and his wife.

'Don't think you can get out of me choosing a shade of purple that'll knock your socks off.' Harper tapped him on the forearm. 'We have a date.' She blinked and gasped as what she'd just said must've sunk in. 'I mean, um, we'll sort out your decorating some time.'

'Let's go sort out accident victims first.' He held the door wide for her, and grinned at the tight back view she presented as she stalked down the corridor, obviously embarrassed with her choice of phrase.

If she hadn't touched a need within him he could've laughed. But she had, and he couldn't. 'Harper? What colour are your eyes?'

He knew when heat touched a face that the shade colouring the cheeks was pink. In this case, bright pink.

She told him in a low voice that sent shivers up his spine and tightened muscles that didn't need tightening right at that moment. 'Brown, with flecks of yellow and green.' She gave him a rueful smile. 'Just so you know.'

CHAPTER SIX

SO MUCH FOR keeping Cody at a safe distance. That question about her eyes was over the top, and warmed her right down to her toes. Her fingers tensed. *And* she'd gone and invited herself to his home—make that *demanded* an invitation—all because she'd been adamant about helping him decide on the colour for his bedroom. Bedroom. Not the bathroom, or kitchen, or dining room. The bedroom. Cody's bedroom.

Yeah, she got it. She'd made a monumental blunder and now had to work out how to backtrack without getting further into deep water. Though he had been reluctant to fix a day or time for her to visit, so that was in her favour if she was serious about changing her mind about helping.

What did it matter to her if he messed up and painted it orange or teal? Or purple? Her mood softened. So the man was colour-blind. He had a fault. A tiny, almost insignificant one, unless he'd wanted to be the captain on one of those fishing trawlers he'd worked on, but it was there. She liked him even more. Damn it.

This time a week ago she'd barely known Cody existed. Now all her spare time was taken up just thinking about him. He filled her skull with questions and nonsense and excitement. She'd even passed the donuts in the break room today without taking one, and she'd made a hair appointment for some highlights and to get the ends tidied. It was an appointment that was long overdue but which hadn't bothered her until—Cody. He was bringing out a side of her she hadn't seen in a very long time.

'You and Cody take Lisa Lang, thirty-one, compound fractures to right leg, possible fractured pelvis. Trauma injury to head. Unconscious.' George stood at the desk organising everyone. 'Resus Two.'

Phew. Not that she'd have time to relive Friday with the patient they were expecting, but so far today she and Cody had managed to avoid Resus One, thanks to George. 'How far out?'

'Next ambulance to arrive. Approximately five minutes.' George called out the names of other nurses to work with them. Then, 'Karin, you take the one after that. I'll be working with you.'

Harper blanked out the rest of George's instructions and concentrated on her patient's requirements. The first of which required a phone call to the on-duty orthopaedic surgeon.

As she did that the bell buzzed, announcing the arrival of their patient, and she saw Cody stride out to the ambulance bay in his fast but seemingly unhurried way.

Then Lisa Lang was wheeled into the room and that was the end of the brief quiet spell.

'GCS and BP?' Harper asked.

'Two and sixty over forty-five.'

'Way too low, even allowing for the fractures and head injury.' Harper issued instructions. 'Cody, IV lines and attach her to the heart monitor. Jess, ABCs. Cath, cut what's left of her clothes away from her chest and that leg for an X-ray. I'm going to intubate.'

Everyone worked fast and efficiently, but it took two attempts for Harper to get the endotracheal tube in place. Finally she was satisfied and straightened up. 'BP?'

'Still sixty over forty-five.'

No change was better than getting worse, but only just. She needed the BP to go up. 'IV?'

'Lines in place, open and running,' Cody told her.

'Right, I need X-rays of the right leg, pelvis and the neck. And a CT scan of that head injury.'

The orthopaedic surgeon walked in as the first image came up on the screen. He tapped the shattered fibula on the screen. 'Now, there's a mess. The tib's looking a little better.'

'BP's seventy over fifty-five,' someone called.

'It's coming up slowly.' Harper answered the surgeon's raised eyebrow and kept working with Lisa until she was taken to pre-op.

But there was no time to catch their breath, as Cody wheeled another patient in from the same vehicular accident. 'Janice Leigh, forty-one, soft head trauma, fractured ribs, possible punctured lung.'

'GCS and BP?' Harper asked. *Here we go again.*

Time flew by and the end of shift seemed to rush at them. By then the last of the victims had been brought in and four of them sent on to Theatre for surgery.

'You've got a chock-full waiting room to deal with.' Harper smiled tiredly at her replacement. 'I'm going home for a long shower, followed by dinner.' A lettuce leaf and tomato. Ah, to hell with it. If her hips were a little heavy, then today she didn't care. Her stomach was crying with need for food, and her energy levels required some input. This was only Monday.

'Some shift that turned out to be,' Cody muttered as he joined her on the walk out of the hospital.

How come he still looked so fresh? Fresh and fit and in very good shape.

Dash. Back to lettuce and tomato. Her determination got a much-needed boost as she observed Cody roaring out of the car park on his motorbike.

What a bod. What a man. What a dilemma.

She could never ask him to give up his need for a family. It wasn't fair. She had to learn to see him as a colleague and nothing more. Had to give up this unexpected need to get closer to him, to get to know him better.

She had to learn not to open her mouth and volunteer dumb things like helping with his home decorating.

Though it would be interesting to see where he lived, and what his taste in housing was. *It's none of your business, Harper!*

Maybe she should buy that board and paddle, head out to sea and never come back, because all she was doing right now was setting herself up for heartbreak. *Concentrate on your work, Harper; that's what's real.* The rest of the week flew by without any major incidents, which for Harper now meant someone holding a loaded gun to her head or the department being swarmed with armed police. The drama of an accident paled in significance, which didn't mean she felt any less concern or worry for her patients. No, they still got to her, had her heart aching for them, as they battled a cardiac arrest, a bleed out or broken bones.

But she felt able to take everything in her stride again—except for walking into Resus One, even when the room was empty; or a curtain being flicked open suddenly; or someone appearing behind her without having made any noise. Those things made her jittery, had her laughing loudly at inopportune moments or dropping a utensil unexpectedly. She'd noticed the same reactions in Jess and Matilda, and had talked to George about getting the young nurses counselling if they wanted it, while turning it down for herself.

The only time she felt completely safe was when Cody was working beside her, his calm demeanour soothing the stress tensing her body.

Now she turned from staring into Resus One to find Cody watching, and said, 'You seem to be coping with the aftermath. How do you do it?'

His smile was soft, contemplative. 'Who says I'm coping?'

'If you're not then you're putting on a good show.'

'That's a relief. I'd hate for everyone to see I'm really just a scaredy-cat.'

As if that would ever happen. The man was fierce in his gaze, in his determination not to be taken down, in his quiet but thorough way of dealing with anything that cropped up. 'Do you wake up during the night in a sweat with your heart pounding? Or leap out of your skin when someone comes into a cubicle far too quietly?'

She hadn't meant to reveal any of that, but around this man her mouth took on a life of its own. She hadn't decided if that was because he was so hot, or so caring, or helpful and understanding. All those attributes and more added to his sexiness, making him one hell of a package that had any cognizant female drooling and acting totally out of character. She was no more immune than any of them. It might be an idea to remember that and accept her feelings for Cody were probably being repeated everywhere.

He said, 'All of that, and other things, like looking

for short men with cold blue eyes in crowds.' It was un-believable how much understanding filtered through his voice.

Her head tipped back and she stared up at him. It wasn't only in his voice, but it was darkening his eyes and softening his expression. No, they had an affinity for each other. She knew it—couldn't deny it any more. What she did about it was up for speculation. She told him, 'I haven't done that.'

'Good. Because once you start looking, there seems to be more creeps out there than you'd ever imagined.' Cody smiled softly, taking the sharpness away from his words. 'But I think I'm getting over it a little. I'm not as edgy as I was on Monday.' So why did his voice hold a hint of tension? Why was it husky and low, goose-bump lifting and spine-tingling raw?

Nothing to do with gangsters.

Harper coughed against her hand, trying to remove the sudden dry tickle at the back of her throat. *Think about the verbal conversation, not the hidden one. Think practical stuff, not hot bodies and sublime re-lease.* 'I'm hoping the weekend off will help, starting at three o'clock this afternoon.' She glanced at her watch. 'In two hours and six minutes, but I'm not counting.'

'Something to be said for Friday nights and week-ends,' he agreed in that voice that was still doing strange things to her insides. Hell, and her outsides—her skin was tightening at the thought of his hands touching her. Huh? When was *that* likely to happen? Not at all, if she had any common sense left, and that was debatable at this moment.

Thank goodness for the two whole days and some hours to do absolutely whatever she chose. Unfortu-nately she couldn't think of anything exciting or distracting that didn't involve Cody. 'What have you got planned for the weekend?' *Shut up.* Ridiculous, how disengaged her brain had become.

Cody's eyes widened slightly and he studied her as though looking for an answer to a question she had no idea about. Then he shrugged oh-so-nonchalantly and picked up a file. 'Not sure.'

'Not painting?' She still hadn't been to his place. Her impatience as she waited for the invitation she knew wouldn't come was getting to her.

'Probably not.' He deliberately glanced down at the paperwork in his hand. 'I'll go and get our next patient.'

Ouch. 'Cubicle Four,' she snapped, not happy at being put in her place. It seemed Cody wasn't having any problems keeping her at a distance after all. She must've imagined those intense looks, or misinterpreted them.

By the time he returned with a man holding a heavily bandaged hand against his chest, Harper had managed to pull on her professional face. 'I'm Dr White. What have you been doing to yourself?' she asked the patient as he settled onto the bed with help from Cody.

'I was replacing a pane of glass in my glasshouse and it slipped through my fingers.' The man winced as he held his hand towards Cody so he could unwrap metres of gauze. 'Silly old coot. My wife always tells me to be careful.'

A quick glance at the patient notes. Sixty-nine... nothing in his medical history to be concerned about. 'I'm sure you were careful, Henry, but accidents do happen. You weren't feeling lightheaded or dizzy when this occurred?'

'Not at all.' He was staring at his hand where all four fingers were sliced on the inside.

As his face turned pale, Cody gently pushed him onto

the pillows. 'Lie back and let Dr White take care of you.' Glancing across to her, he added, 'I'll get the suture kit.'

The curtain flicked behind him as he strode out. His face had been inscrutable, not an expression she was used to seeing when it came to Cody. Looking at her watch, she sighed. One hour and fifty-eight minutes of cold shoulder to get through. His sudden mood change annoyed her. What was so damn wrong with asking about his weekend plans?

'How bad is it?' Henry asked as she gently prised his fingers open again and studied the wounds.

'The cuts don't appear to have gone too deep but I'm going to put stitches in each finger. You won't be using this hand for a few days.'

Henry didn't look too unhappy. 'Will you give me something for the pain, doc?'

Her head shot up and she glared around the cubicle. Doc. He was here. The gunman had returned.

A large, gentle hand settled between her shoulder blades. 'Easy, *Doctor* White. Harper.'

Cody's calm tone instantly returned her to normal and brought her back into the cubicle with a man dressed in his gardening clothes, requiring sutures, waiting patiently on the bed, unaware of the shock he'd given her. Her breath sighed over her bottom lip. 'Thanks.'

Cody's mouth softened, and the corners lifted enough to show that everything was all right between them. His voice was low and husky as he told her, 'I've got your back, Harper.'

There really was no escaping the fact they were more than colleagues, not when he looked and spoke like that. Suddenly she let it all go, gave up trying to pretend she had to keep him at arm's length. Her heart lifted, expanded and warmth trickled throughout her body. Her eyes also got in on the act, getting a bit wet, and she hurriedly had to wipe her forearm over them. 'I know.' She did too. Even while feeling that resurging fear she'd known Cody would be there for her.

'Do I need antibiotics?' her patient asked, bringing her back to reality.

No, that wasn't true. She was already there. Whatever was going on between her and Cody, it was real. She found a smile for Henry. 'Yes, and a painkiller.'

She got on with stitching the injured fingers: the only sewing she found interesting and actually ever finished, she acknowledged with wry amusement. That pile on her table at home was destined for the bin, or to go to someone who'd actually enjoy working with the fabrics.

Cody returned to the cubicle after showing Henry out, flicking the curtain closed. 'At the risk of being turned down again, I'm going to extend the same invitation as I did last Friday. Want to go for a drink with all the crew when we're done here?'

'I'd love to.'

Surprise registered in those green eyes, lightening them to her favourite shade—spring grass. 'Good,' he muttered, his gaze firmly fixed on her.

So firmly she felt as though he was boring into her, seeing behind all the nonsense she put out there to try and keep him at a distance. The longer and harder he watched her, the softer and warmer she felt. Her mouth formed one word. 'Cody.'

One step and he was there, right in front of her, only inches separating them. 'Harper.' His hand lifted to her cheek, his finger tracing a delicate line down to her mouth, along her lips, then down over her chin, where he applied gentle pressure to tilt her head back. 'Harper,' he whispered close to her mouth, before his lips covered hers softly.

Her mouth opened under his, letting his tongue in to taste her, to allow her to taste him. She'd been reliving that first kiss all week, and it hadn't come close to the real thing. Soft went to possessive and demanding and their tongues danced around each other's; her heart rate shot through the roof while her body folded in against the hard wall of muscle that was Cody. His hands held her head. Her hands splayed over his forearms. His chest pressed against her breasts which ached where her nipples pushed against him.

'Oops, sorry. Warning—incoming patient.' Karin's voice slammed into the haze that Cody's kiss had brought over her. The curtain brackets slid noisily over the bar as Karin left them alone.

Harper stilled and pulled her mouth away from that kiss so slowly it took a while to notice she was no longer touching his lips. She sank onto the bed behind her, her legs no longer capable of doing what they were supposed to. Her eyes felt enormous, probably looking like headlights on a car.

Cody looked just as shocked. Or was that pleased with himself? His eyes had caught the same wide, staring bug hers had. That beautiful mouth that had devoured hers was curving up into a smile that had her heart beating even harder, more than she'd have thought possible. Could she be in danger of a cardiac malfunction?

She stared up at this man who turned her world upside down as easily as most men pulled on their pants in the morning. 'Wow.'

He grinned. Then a low laugh erupted from him.

'Yeah, wow.' His hand cupped her face, his thumb tracing her lips. 'Guess we'd better act like we're working.'

'There is a patient on the way.'

'There is.'

'He or she will need this bed.'

'And your doctoring skills and my nursing ones.' His smile widened.

'Did that really just happen? At work?' Where anyone could've burst in on them? Thank goodness it'd been Karin.

'Yep.'

Damn. Wow. Hell. What now? They'd stepped over the mark and there'd be no going back. Or if they tried to it wouldn't be easy to return to their former 'doctor and nurse' relationship. *Huh? You haven't strictly had that for a week now.*

Cody dropped his hand and stepped back. 'You're over-thinking it. Don't,' he warned before pushing the curtain open and looking out for their patient.

He was right. As always. 'That drink at the pub?'

He stilled, his hand gripping a bunch of curtain. He didn't say a word, merely waited.

'Think we can leave our vehicles here for the night and have more than one glass?' *And maybe get back to kissing at some point.* She'd sell her soul for another of those mind-blowing, knee-bending kisses.

His smile was slow, sexy and full of promise. At least, that was how she interpreted it. 'That's what taxis are for.'

'Right, in here.' Karin's voice was raised and there was a pause before she brought her patient in.

Harper tried not to look at her but it wasn't easy. Finally deciding to get it over with, she locked eyes with the registrar, as though to say, *So what? You caught us kissing. Big deal.* A massive deal, in fact. But Karin didn't need to know that.

'Well, well, well,' the registrar muttered so only she heard. 'What was it you said last week? "Not interested", I think. Hate to see you in action when you are.'

'Shut it, Karin,' Harper growled, or tried to, but only managed to splutter on a laugh.

'My lips are sealed. Unlike someone else's.' She winked and turned to the teenager she'd shown into the cubicle. 'Tell me about this abdominal pain. When did it start?'

Cody stayed with Karin as she diagnosed probable appendicitis when the girl admitted to pains in her right side. He drew some bloods for a CBC and CRP which would confirm if there was an inflammation of the appendix. He sat with the girl when she had a crying spell at the thought of 'going under the knife', as she put it.

All the while Harper cruised through his mind, never leaving, always reminding him of that kiss and how much he wanted to follow up on it. Just as he had on Sunday and all week since. Sheesh. A kiss was a kiss, but Harper's kisses were something else. Off the planet. Mind-shattering. Body-crunching. Full of promise. *I have to have her. As soon as possible.*

The thermometer he'd read after taking the girl's temperature hit the floor and shattered. His neck cricked at the sudden hard movement he made in response.

You what?

Have to take Harper to bed. Today, tonight.

This was not meant to happen. They were supposed to remain professional, with a little bit of friendship added in for good measure after all they'd been through together.

So why did I kiss her?

What choice did he have? As if he could've ignored that look in her eyes or dodged that welcoming, delicious mouth that had tormented him since their first kiss.

'Nurse Brand, you going to sweep up that glass today?' Karin was grinning from across the bed.

Dropping his head forward, he stared at the mess at his feet. Shoving a hand through his hair, he felt his gut tighten in disbelief. What an idiot. 'On my way to the cleaning cupboard.'

Karin poked her head out of the curtains to whisper after him as he left, 'I think Dr White is in Cubicle One, which is on the way to that cupboard.' Laughter laced the registrar's voice and grated on Cody's nerves.

'We'd prefer it if you could keep what you saw to yourself,' he ground out through clenched teeth.

'Relax, Cody. No one will learn anything from me. But you do realise everyone's already watching the pair of you? We might still be getting to know you, but the same can't be said for Harper.'

'Meaning?'

'That she's acting different these days. More out there and less control-freak mode.'

Really? Because of him? That'd be…wonderful. Cody swore under his breath. 'Has anyone considered she's still coming to terms with last Friday's incident and is having some major moments where it all comes back to her in full colour?'

Consternation flicked across Karin's face. 'I thought she was handling it amazingly well.' Then she lightened up again. 'I still think you're cheering her up immensely.'

'I need a broom.' He stomped off, not sure whether

he should be happy or annoyed about that last comment. Having Harper happy because of him—yes, he could go with that. Wanted to. He thought about her all the time. It seemed that, whether he was ready or not, he was stepping out into the risk pool because he more than liked her.

Which brought him right back to kissing Harper. *Amazing.* It definitely needed repeating. He paused at Cubicle One. The curtain was open and it would be rude to ignore the doctor standing beside the bed. Especially as she was looking straight out at him. 'Hey,' he said. 'You okay?'

'More than,' she responded in a hurry, and glanced at her watch. 'One hour and five.'

'That's for ever,' he muttered and headed away. If he'd thought working with Harper prior to that kiss had been hard, he hadn't had a clue. Kissing her outside of work was one thing, but now the department was no longer a no-go zone. Now… Now he wanted to haul her back into his arms and kiss her until she melted against him; kiss her senseless; kiss her until they were hauling off clothes and getting skin to skin. Hot, slick skin to hot, slick skin. Definitely not to be done in the department.

But there were other places.

CHAPTER SEVEN

THE PUB WAS CROWDED, even out in the garden bar. 'It's only just gone three-thirty,' Cody grumped as he placed a laden tray on the table, where eight of the day shift sat in various states of relaxation.

'It's twenty-six degrees outside, the drinks are cold and there's a one-day cricket game on the screen. Where else would anyone want to be?' Harper asked before sipping the Pinot Gris he'd bought her.

'You prefer your sport from a chair, don't you?'

'Safer that way. You've seen what happened to my knees at tennis. There's also a bruise on my thigh from a misdirected cricket ball last Sunday.'

'Not misdirected at all. You were supposed to catch it.'

Sitting on the bench seat beside her, he stretched his legs under the table, then shuffled his butt to move closer. Feeling her length against his leg, he sighed with pleasure. What could be better than this? *Taking her to bed.*

Jerking sideways, he shook the table, which sent waves of beer and wine slopping over the tops of the glasses and earned him a bunch of wisecracks from everyone. Everyone except Harper. She just stared at him with a half-smile on that mouth he wanted to claim, and a very knowing gleam in her eyes.

'I shouted the round. I'm allowed to knock things sideways. Okay, guys?' He grinned around at them all and picked up his beer. 'Cheers.' *And stop staring at me like I've grown another head, or as if I might've got too close to Harper.* He swallowed beer too fast, gasped and had to suffer the mortification of being slapped on the back by her.

'Harder, Harper. Give him what for. Cheeky so-and-so needs keeping in line.'

'Go, girl. Bang him between the shoulder blades. Yep, that's good.'

Bang him? Wrong phrase, Jess.

Harper must have picked up on the unintentional innuendo because she sat back in a hurry. 'Just trying to help a man in need.' She was rubbing her palms together, slowly, as if feeling something. Was she sensing his muscles under her hand?

In need? He certainly was. His glass slammed onto the table. *Wishful thinking, buddy.* He glanced at her face. *Or maybe not.* Looking around the table, he cringed as he met the steady and amused looks from each and every damned one of their colleagues. 'Who's up for a game of darts?' he asked and stood up abruptly.

The invitation is not extended to you, Harper.

Considering her lack of co-ordination when it came to anything sporty, he doubted she'd want to be throwing a sharp dart anywhere, so everyone was safe. Except him. He needed her to remain on that bench, drinking her wine and pretending he wasn't here. Then these knuckleheads might get on with their afternoon without stirring things up for Harper or him.

'I will.' Jess picked up her beer and followed him inside to the board. 'You any good at this?'

'Yeah, a little.' Champion of the local pub in Invercargill for three years running.

'Then we've got ourselves a game.' Jess laughed as she picked up the darts and handed him a set.

He'd go easy on her to start. He held a coin ready to toss. 'Heads or tails?'

Forty minutes later, he shook his head at Jess and said, 'My shout. You play a mean game.' She'd beaten his hide, well and truly. He saw Harper heading out from the bathroom. 'You want another wine?'

'Please. Outside again?' Harper asked. 'It's a little cooler out there. Though with the after-work crowd arriving it's getting crowded.'

'We could go find somewhere quieter,' he suggested hopefully after giving the order to the barman.

'Haven't you been trying to divert everyone's attention off us this past three-quarters of an hour?' Harper's smile twisted his gut.

'You're right. Okay, back into the fray.'

'I'm enjoying this.' She slipped her arm through his.

Instinctively he squeezed his arm to bring her hand hard against his ribs. Then gulped. 'Don't,' he said quietly.

Jerking her hand free she muttered, 'Sorry, don't know what I was thinking.'

'I think you do, but we are supposed to be acting like colleagues, nothing else.' Harper had to be the sensible one. He was beyond it.

A group of suits pushed past them, knocking Harper sideways. Catching her around the waist to prevent her falling, he growled, 'Watch where you're going, guys,' and got glared at for his trouble.

'Says who?' asked one smart-ass as he gave Cody the once-over and obviously found him wanting, probably because he wasn't togged up in a white shirt and business suit.

Harper slipped her hand into his and tugged him sideways. 'Leave them.' She took a long drink from her glass and placed it back on the counter, took his drink from him and put that beside hers. Then she headed for the main entrance, pulling him along with her.

'Where might we be going?'

'Your place or mine?' Harper grinned, though apprehension did cross her eyes briefly. 'I'm over pretending we want to be here, playing nice.'

What? 'Just like that?' Had he heard right? 'You're sure?'

Twisting her head to one side, she eyed him coolly. 'You have to ask?'

'Just checking.' He'd hate to get it wrong. 'Your apartment. It's closer.' Barely, but the sudden tightening making itself felt in his boxers needed dealing with—fast.

The sun blinded him when they staggered outside. A taxi was dropping off more punters and he waved furiously to get the driver's attention. Bundling Harper inside, he rattled off her address to the driver and sat back against her, draping his arm over her shoulders. What had just happened? One moment they were agreeing they had to be sensible around the others and then, wham, they were in a cab heading for Harper's apartment. *Can you drive this thing any faster, mate? I'm getting a little worked up back here.*

Harper laid her head on his shoulder, lifted it almost immediately and turned so she could place her mouth on his. 'It's not too late to tell me this is a crazy idea and that we should stop.'

It had been too late hours ago. From the moment he'd leaned in to steal a kiss in Cubicle Four, it'd been all over. They'd always been going to follow through after that. Not that in a million years he'd thought they'd be heading for Harper's apartment quite this soon.

When the taxi turned into her street, his heart rate shot through the stratosphere. Nearly there. Then the fun could really start.

Suddenly Harper sat up straight and cried out to the driver, 'Turn around. We need to go somewhere else. Cody, what's your address?'

Cody felt he'd been punched in the gut. 'What? Why? We're here.' *And I can't wait much longer to tear your clothes off and hold your naked body against mine, and...*

'Suzanne and Steve are in my apartment. We can't stop here.'

Too late. The taxi was slowing against the kerb right at the end of the path that led to Harper's open front door where Suzanne was turning to look their way.

Cody began hauling the brakes on his desire. It seemed they weren't about to get naked together. Not here, anyway.

Harper said, 'I totally forgot they'd be here. They're going to an awards dinner in the city and didn't want to drive home after.' Her look was imploring. 'Give the driver your address. Now.'

Cody pulled back from her a little. 'You can't drive away without stopping in. Suzanne's seen us pull up. She's going to be upset if you don't at least say hello.'

Harper pulled a face. 'Talk about throwing cold water on the moment. Please take me to your place.'

The driver was watching them through the rear-view mirror, the grin on his face suggesting he was completely up to date with the situation.

'Shortly.' He reached across Harper to open her door. 'Your sister is looking mighty puzzled at the moment.'

Harper's face shut down. 'Why didn't you just tell the driver where to go? I don't need to see my sister right now.' She didn't move at all.

'Are you ashamed to be seen with me?' Because, if she was, he was gone. Right now. To hell with how he felt about her or how much he wanted her.

'What?' Stunned didn't begin to describe her face. 'No.' Then louder. 'No.' Then a shout. 'No. Not at all.'

Relief poured through him. 'Then what's this about?'

'You know what they're like. They'll give me grief for days. The phone calls won't stop. The texts will get cheekier.'

'From what I've seen of your family, you all tease each other mercilessly over absolutely everything. You and I together for a night isn't something out of the ordinary.' Yes, it was, for a totally different reason. 'What I mean is, it's no different to them teasing you about that pathetic toss of the ball at the wickets last Sunday.'

Harper's mouth lifted a little from the flat line she'd been holding it in. 'I guess you're right.' Shoving the door wide, she slid out. 'Be right back.'

'What are you going to say?' he called after her. Beyond her, he saw Steve join his wife.

'I've come to get my toothbrush.'

Cody cursed. 'Keep the meter running,' he told the driver, grateful that his excitement had backed off enough not to be obvious to everyone. 'Be right back.'

'What are you doing?' Harper asked as he caught up to her.

'Getting the toothpaste.' He wasn't going sit in the car while she talked to her family. That would make him look gutless or rude, and he was neither. Nor was he ashamed of whatever he and Harper were going to get up to tonight.

Harper rewarded him with a grin before acknowledging her family. 'Hey, guys, thought you'd be downing cocktails at that swanky hotel already.'

'Obviously.' Suzanne smirked. 'Nothing gets underway for another hour, but if you'd like us to get out of your way then I'm sure we can find somewhere to fill in time. Hi, Cody. Good to see you again,' she purred with a mischievous glint in her eyes.

Jeez. Maybe he should've stayed in the taxi. 'Same back to you both.'

Harper slipped between them and headed down the hall, calling over her shoulder, 'Just grabbing a couple of things.'

Like what? Cody wondered, considering they'd headed this way to get undressed, not dressed up.

'Not staying for a drink, then?' Suzanne called after her.

Harper came straight back. 'You shouldn't be drinking. You're pregnant.'

'Strictly orange juice for me. But thought you might want to join Steve in a beer. If you've got time, that is.'

Cody felt laughter beginning to rise up his throat. These White girls knew how to wind each other up something awful and didn't care who else they caught in the web. He turned to Steve. 'Do they ever let up?'

'Better get used to it.' The guy nodded, then added, 'If you're hanging around, that is.'

'Jeez, you're no better.' He should've done as Harper

had demanded and told the taxi driver to turn around while he'd had the chance. Was he hanging around? Did he want to spend time with Harper? Time beyond today and what they were heading for at his house? Yes. Yes. Oh, hell, yes.

Steve chuckled. 'The White family is not for the faint-hearted.'

Right now Cody couldn't give a damn about his heart, faint or not. All he wanted was Harper in his arms so he could do things with her that no one else need know about. 'That meter's ticking over,' he called down the hall.

Suzanne added, 'He's impatient, Harper. Better get a move on.'

Steve just chuckled again and headed inside. 'I'm having my beer.'

Harper burst out the door, nothing more in her hand than the handbag she'd carried inside. 'Have a great night, you two.'

Get in, be seen to do the right thing and get out: Cody couldn't argue with that. He caught her elbow and started down the path. 'See you, Suzanne, Steve.'

'We'll see you at Levi's party,' Suzanne said.

'Maybe,' he muttered, and got a quizzical look from the woman he was hurrying towards the taxi. 'One thing at a time,' he told her.

Tonight was about Harper. And him. And that incredible need cranking up again with every step he took away from the nosey sister. Getting Harper into the cab made him hum. Giving the driver his address caused him to pause for a breath, then shrug. He'd already admitted to himself he was more than interested in furthering their relationship. Letting her into his home was another step in the right direction.

* * *

Cody's solid timber front door closed with a heavy thud behind them, and Harper gazed around at the wide entrance with massive painted pots filled with flowers placed strategically on either side. 'Those are beautiful.' The house was massive. She'd been wrong to think he'd bought a starter house. Unless he was aiming for a castle some time.

'Did I get the colours right, then?' Cody asked with a little hitch in his voice.

'Did you choose these?' Had he been winding her up about being colour-blind? She turned to look closely at him, wondering about that hitch, and saw nothing but pride in his expression.

'The pots are my mother's. She had them for years, since before they were fashionable. Dad gave them to her for their thirtieth wedding anniversary. Unfortunately there's nowhere for them in her room at the rest home. These need space to be appreciated. As for the flowers, I get the local florist to take care of those.' His chest lifted on a deep breath, drawing her gaze and reminding her why they were here.

As if she needed reminding, when her body was ramped up and in hot turmoil. Her heart hadn't stopped its heavy tattoo since they'd been in the pub. Not even seeing that smug, knowing look on Suzanne's face had quietened it down. There'd been a moment when they'd first pulled up outside her apartment when the heat in her belly had cooled a weeny bit. But one look at Cody, one word spoken in that husky voice, the slightest of touches from his hand and arm and, pow…where were the fans? She flapped her hand in front of her face. Her body needed relief. Relief of the kind that only a man could give, a man built like a sex god. Not any sex god either. Cody. The one and only. To hell with vases and flowers.

Harper reached for him.

He grasped her, those hands heavy and hot on her waist.

Pulling at his shirt, she pushed it up over that magnificent expanse of chest so she could see it, feel it, without the hindrance of clothing. His body was better than her imagination had conjured up.

Cody tugged at her blouse, pulling it free of her skirt, taking it up and over her head, his gaze fixed on her lace-covered breasts. Thank goodness she'd left her plain, sensible bras in the drawer that morning.

Leaning in, she kissed a trail over the warm skin tempting her. She started with one nipple and worked her way across to its opposite number, tasting, sipping, enjoying.

His fingers slid up under her bra, found her breasts and cupped them while his thumbs flicked back and forth over her taut nipples.

It wasn't enough. Her body craved Cody's. All of Cody's. Against her, inside her, with her. Her fingers worked the button of his chinos, then the fly that strained against the throbbing, hard heat pushing between them. Then he was filling her hands with all that hot length. Her fingers wound around his shaft, tightened, loosened, tightened.

Above her head, Cody gasped. His hands groped for her skirt, found the zip and jerked it down, shoving at it until it slid over her hips to pool at her feet. Then she was in his arms, being lifted and turned so her back was against the wall.

Winding her legs around his waist and her arms behind his head, Harper lifted her mouth to his. He was ready for her, his lips swollen and demanding. As she closed her eyes, Harper wondered if she'd fallen into a deep dream. This was beyond great, beyond anything she *could* dream of. The male scent of Cody's skin filled her nostrils. Those large, strong hands held her tight yet easy. They touched, teased, tweaked, caressed. They drove her to the edge in a very short time.

Pulling her mouth free, she managed a strangled, 'Cody...' before he claimed her again, giving more kisses, taking hers in return. Whatever she'd been about to say was whisked away in a haze of need.

She couldn't wait any longer. Her throbbing, moist sex was way past ready. 'Please,' she begged as her hands found him again, pushing his boxers aside.

'Wait.'

She couldn't.

'Condom,' he wheezed through gritted teeth. 'Pocket. Trousers.'

How was it that his chinos hadn't slid down to his ankles? Not enough movement could be the problem. She grinned under his mouth. Her fingers dug into his back pocket and thankfully it was the right one. She mightn't be able to last long enough to do a search of every pocket on those trousers.

'Hold on.' Cody tore open the packet with his teeth.

Wrapping her arms around his neck and tightening her grip with her legs, she obeyed. And then...then... He was filling her, with heat and movement, himself.

She'd been mad to think she could go without Cody even for the past week. She'd wasted days. Tipping her head back hard against the wall, she gave into the sensations tripping and ripping through her; gave in to the need clawing at her insides; gave in to Cody's hot demands and accepted his gift as he made love to her as she'd never been made love to before.

Cody scooped Harper up into his arms from where they'd finished up sprawled over the floor, precariously close to one of those massive pottery urns. 'Let's make ourselves comfortable,' he murmured near her ear and headed for the stairs that led to his bedroom.

'Mmm.' She barely moved, her eyelids stayed closed, but that delicious—yep, now he knew how delicious— mouth curved up into a beautiful smile that sent warmth spearing at his heart.

Whoa. His heart had nothing to do with what had just gone down between them. That would be plain dumb. No matter how great the sex was, how well they got on, what if he gave her his heart and he lost her? He couldn't guarantee he could survive that a second time. He'd believed after Sadie had been killed that nothing similar would happen to him again. Then along had come Strong and the body packer. Terrifying. Did violence follow him? What if something occurred he couldn't protect Harper from? He'd failed with Sadie. He wouldn't risk not getting it right for this surprise package in his arms. She didn't deserve his mistakes.

Harper's lips grazed his jaw, her tongue flicking over his lips, turning up his blood to race along his veins.

Now is not the time for this, his inner voice snapped. *Enjoy, have fun, forget consequences. Just go with the moment.*

Not a bad plan, he admitted. At the door of his bedroom, he paused. 'Now you get to tell me what colour to decorate in here.'

Her eyes slowly opened and she peered around. 'This is a bedroom? It's the size of my whole apartment.' Her head came up off his chest as she tried to take in more. 'Cripes. I don't believe what I'm seeing.' She snuggled down against him again, her eyes now shut and her mouth still smiling. 'I knew I was dreaming.'

Cody laughed as he gently laid Harper on the bed before crossing to open the windows and let some air in. The room pretty much got all-day sun, which on a day when the temperature had been high made it a furnace.

A light sea breeze obliged him, sending soft tendrils of cooler air over his skin. 'Feel that?' he asked as he lay down beside this woman who had him all shaken up. Or was that all melted down?

'It's wonderful. So is that finger you're trailing over my breast.' Totally uninterested in where she was, and only in what he was doing to her body, she stretched like a cat, her arms above her head, her feet reaching to the bottom of the bed. They were never going to find it, the bed being super-king-sized and Harper being about five-six.

But, now that he'd relaxed again and put other things out of his head, he loved watching those cute feet with their—blue?—nails moving back and forth across the cover. 'What colour's your nail polish?'

'Dark pink.'

'Not blue, then.'

Those eyes he'd grown very fond of twinkled with mirth. 'Nowhere near, buster.'

'For what it's worth, I like dark-pink-slash-blue.' He stretched out on his side beside Harper and draped an arm over her waist. 'It would look good on these walls.'

Her eyes widened and the twinkles just got brighter. 'Very masculine, I'm sure. You could have light pink curtains to match. Duvet in pink and white. Yes, I can see it now.' Her gaze roamed the room and her expression got a little serious. 'What an amazing space. You can do so much with this.'

'Starting with showcasing the view. I'm planning on bigger, lower windows so I can see out over the bay while lying in bed.' He still pinched himself that he'd been able to purchase this property. There'd been two other buyers trying to outbid him, but once he'd started he'd had to have it. He'd probably spent tens of thousands too many but as he intended staying put for the foreseeable future he knew it was money well spent. As long as he got the renovations right, as well as the colour scheme.

Harper was giggling. Giggling? What happened to serious? Now very immature and absolutely loveable. 'Don't make those windows too low or you won't be able to do anything interesting in this bed without an audience. Even if you are two storeys up.'

There was his cue, if he needed one. 'Then we'd better make the most of how things are at the moment.'

'I like the way you think.' She rolled into him, all soft, pliant and utterly desirable.

Would he ever be able to get enough of her? He hoped so or he was in trouble. 'Lie back and enjoy. This is your moment.'

'But I want to play too.'

'Oh, Harper, you're going to play, believe me.' And he proceeded to show her exactly what he meant.

Harper rolled over and put a forearm over her eyes to blot out the sunlight streaming in through the windows. Her body ached pleasurably everywhere, even in places she hadn't known existed until now. Not that she was complaining. Not at all. They were delicious aches. This had to be the best way ever invented to wake up. Shaking her head, she stifled a laugh. She'd got it bad. Got Cody bad. Crikey, but he'd delivered, more than once. More than twice. Even after taking time out for food, because they'd needed sustenance to carry on *playing*, he'd known how to keep her keen and willing. The man rocked.

She grinned and stretched, making herself as long as possible, reaching for each end of the bed and not quite making it. Maybe she'd finally found her hobby. One that didn't give her grazes or bruises, or bored her senseless.

'What's making you look so satisfied with yourself?'

'Oh, you know. It's Saturday and I'm not going to work. The sun's shining and the wind hasn't come up yet. I've got nothing I have to do by any specific time.'

'Zero to do with amazing sex, then. I get it.' Cody stood at the end of the bed, grinning down at her, that well-honed body just as mouth-watering now as it had been the first time she'd seen it. 'You won't be wanting your messages, then.' He held out her phone.

'Where did that get to?' She pushed up against the pillows and took it to scroll through the latest texts.

'Behind a flower pot and under these.' He held up her panties and swung them on one finger. 'Just as well we haven't reached the technological age where our phone screens automatically show the view.'

'Drat. I forgot to cancel that.'

'Cancel what?' The bed dipped as Cody sat down beside her.

'A paddle-board. I was going to give it a go but changed my mind.' She felt a little sheepish as his eyes widened and a laugh rumbled over his tongue.

'You what?'

'I figured if I fell off…make that *when* I fell off…I'd

have a soft landing and no scrapes or bruises.' She stared out at the sparkling blue-green harbour and shook her head. 'But why spend all that money when I know I'll only give up after the first attempt? I don't have a sports bone in my body.' She could give the board to the kids.

'I beg to differ. You can be very athletic when you find the right activity.'

When she caught his gaze, she saw amusement gleaming out at her and she blushed. 'Didn't even graze my knees.' Her eyes cruised over him and stopped at his scratched upper arms. *Gulp.* 'Did I do that?' She couldn't have.

'Yep.'

Contrition jarred her. 'I'm sorry,' she muttered. 'I don't... Haven't... Sorry,' she repeated lamely and stared at her fingernails. She must've been out of her mind with desire. Yeah, she had been. Cody had driven her over the edge easily, often, and she couldn't be held responsible for her actions.

'Hey.' A large hand covered both hers. 'What's a few light scratches in the heat of the moment? I didn't notice until I got under the shower and added soap to the mix.'

'Now, there's a thought. A shower.' Her muscles were in need of a warm soak—a long one, at that.

'Help yourself. There're towels on the heated rail. Want to stroll down to Oriental Parade after and find somewhere to have breakfast?'

'Sounds perfect.'

But as she stood under the jets of hot water she couldn't help wondering where this was going. One night of sex, the best sex ever, didn't change everything. She still had to work with Cody afterwards. She still couldn't give him children—which was getting way too far ahead of things. She still couldn't trust her heart to anyone either, not even Cody. Again, getting way too ahead of herself. Or was she? The feelings rolling through her at the moment were warm, soft, happy and…exciting.

Rinsing the knots out of her hair, she lathered Cody's shampoo through while her mind worked overtime. She was definitely getting way ahead of herself. She'd done that with Darren and had believed everything was working out perfectly. She needed to take a back step to protect herself, remind herself what the future held, because already it was apparent she couldn't have a few nights of sex with Cody and wave goodbye as she'd done with the two previous sexual encounters she'd indulged in since her marriage had caved.

A few nights? Who'd said anything about any more nights together? Neither of them had, but there hadn't been time. Easy enough to remedy. She'd started the ball rolling yesterday when she'd hauled him out of the pub. She could, and would, do something similar today if necessary, and somehow she didn't think Cody was finished with her yet.

She reached blindly for hair conditioner and opened her eyes. None. Damn. Her hair felt hard and icky with only shampoo through it. *Suck it up.* There wouldn't be a blow-dryer either. *Bad hair day coming up.*

Snapping off the water, she reached for a towel, soft, large and smelling of aloe vera. Rubbing her nose against the soft weave, she sighed with pleasure. So the man had taste in towels and soap powder. And she had it real bad. *Forget it, Harper. He's not for keeps.* He could be, if she'd had what he needed, but she didn't.

So, should she dry off, shuck back into yesterday's clothes and head out the front door with a casual wave and a *thanks for the great sex, see you on Monday* tossed over her shoulder?

Something like that made a lot of sense.

She always did sensible these days.

A little gremlin woke up fast. *So don't. Be different. Instigate more sex later today. Accept what you can't change and go for whatever you want anyway.*

That could end up with someone getting hurt. Cody. Or her. But the idea of having a relationship expanded as fast as she tried to push it away. After Darren, she'd believed she'd be single for the rest of her life unless she found a man over eighty who didn't want children interrupting his sleep, and she still thought that. But her conversation with Jason echoed somewhere in the back of her mind. Maybe she could have a different dream. What she could do, and it seemed really wanted to do, was have fun with a man. Not only in bed, or on the floor in the entranceway, but over breakfast on the Parade, going to the movies, playing cricket together with the brat pack, or spending time with her family and getting teased silly. Or choosing paint colours.

'You going to be all day?' Cody leaned against the doorframe, hands in his jeans pockets, for all appearances like he had the whole day to wait for her. 'You left the door open.'

She hadn't noticed. Warmth stole through her. Not rampaging heat that ended in an orgasm, but soft heat that touched her heart, her toes, her tummy and all places in between. He made her feel good about herself. Not something she'd experienced for a long time. For too long. 'I don't suppose you've got a drawer full of make-up anywhere?'

'I'm all out of it. You'll have to go completely natural, which is better than being plastered with goo anyway.'

That softness intensified. He paid the nicest compliments, even if not quite true. 'Then I'm nearly done.' She looked around the bathroom. 'You thinking about any changes in here?'

Cody nodded. 'There's not a room that doesn't need dealing with. I'll give you the grand tour before we head out.'

'The house appears huge.'

'It is.' He grinned. 'I visited when I was fourteen and in the rugby team. The coach owned it, and I've wanted something like it ever since.'

'You got the real deal.'

'Wanting this place is what started me on the property ladder. A fishing mate and I saved hard to go halves in a rundown shack that we could rent out. Soon we mortgaged it to the hilt and bought another, and then another, until…' his grin widened. '…here I am. Back in Wellington in the house of my teenaged dreams.'

'Go you.' She gazed out of the window at the harbour sparkling in the sun, absorbing how much he'd told her about himself. 'You'll never get tired of looking at that.'

'I agree. Even the windy days are wonderful. Then there are the ferries scooting back and forth, and the fishing fleet heading out to the Strait. It's great.' He was almost purring.

As they wandered along the Parade hand in hand Cody said, 'I'm thinking we should hire two paddleboards and give it a crack before you cancel that order. This could be the one sport you're great at.'

The sea was so calm she couldn't use that as an excuse. 'I haven't got any gear with me and I'm not immersing this skirt in salt water.'

'I'd have enjoyed watching as it got wet and figure-hugging.' He gave an exaggerated sigh. 'Not my lucky day. I could offer you one of my tee-shirts but that'd be all over the place on you, no figure-hugging going on at all. We'll have to drop by your place. You think those other two will still be there once we've had breakfast?'

'I have no idea.' She batted his arm lightly. 'You make it sound as though we're definitely following through on your idea of paddle-boarding.' Her problem being...? Didn't she want to have fun with him? Hadn't she been extolling the reasons she should let go and enjoy life?

'Relax. Your knees will be fine.'

They mightn't have got the skin scraped off them, but they were going to hurt like stink tomorrow, Harper decided as she stiffened into a slight turn three hours later. Breakfast had been long and leisurely, then there'd been coffee with Suzanne and Steve in her tiny back yard. Now finally they were on the water, and she was wobbling front, backwards and sideways, feeling like a drunk penguin. 'Keeping my balance is hard work,' she growled as Cody came close.

'Relax into the movement of the board, don't fight it.'

Easy for him to say. 'Go away. You're causing waves.' *Show off.* Just because he could do this without even trying. *So unfair.* She'd have to challenge him to a knitting contest next. Except she barely knew one end of a knitting needle from the other.

Damn, but he looked good wet. Those board shorts clung to his butt and thighs, making her mouth moist and her tummy tight. As for his chest... She'd never been a chest girl before but Cody was breaking all her norms.

Now he grinned at her. 'Waves are when water rises above the level.'

She didn't deign to supply him with a reply. Instead

she pushed the paddle deeper and pulled on the handle to move forward. Her arms were starting to complain about this added activity too. Paddling was definitely more strenuous than inserting IV lines or stitching wounds.

She snuck another sideways glance and had to stare. Cody standing on his board, looking for all the world as if he'd been born doing this, was a picture to remember. He had natural balance. 'How come you're so relaxed with this?' She could see his calf muscles adjusting as the board beneath his feet shifted. Unlike hers, which were tight and unyielding to any movement.

'Comes from years of staying upright on the deck of a heaving trawler.' Cody pushed the paddle through the water, his strokes effortless. Didn't she know it? Her face heated as memories of the previous night flooded her brain.

'Want to head back to shore?' Mr Oh-So-Good-at-This cruised close again. 'I'll shout you a cold drink.'

'And an ice-cream.' What had happened to the diet? *Tomorrow.* She began working the board around to face the shore—or make that she began *trying* to head home—but the current had changed and she wasn't going anywhere in the direction she needed to.

'Now I know where the brats get their love of ice-cream. They're copying Auntie Harper.'

A wave passed under her board and she froze, afraid to move in case she got it wrong and overbalanced. 'That's a proper wave,' she muttered through clenched teeth.

'Hey,' Cody was yelling. 'Back off. Can't you morons see what we're doing here?'

Harper risked twisting her head to the left to see who had caused his annoyance and her decidedly wobbly ride, and saw a speed boat about a hundred metres away going full throttle and sending out huge bow waves.

Slosh. Slosh. Water rushed at her, over her feet, and continued into shore. 'Do I paddle or freeze? Do I try to keep moving while balancing like a stork?'

The left side of the board lifted. Uh-oh. Her hands gripped the paddle handle. *Like that's going to help,* she thought as she leaned into the lift. The board dropped back flat while her momentum took her head-first into the tide.

Thunk. As she popped upwards, pain blasted into her skull. The board? It had to be. She kicked hard, hopefully away from it, and surfaced—to get a swipe on the chin from the paddle she'd let go as she'd fallen in. *Ow. Pick on me, why don't you?*

'Harper? You all right?' Cody straddled his board, reaching out to her, concern etching his face.

'My knees are fine.' She spluttered out a mouthful of salt water. 'Yuk. That's gross.'

'Those morons should've been driving their boat a lot slower. There are speed restrictions around here,' Cody muttered as he concentrated on getting her sorted. Catching her hand, he tugged her close to his board, hers following as the cord attached to both her ankle and the back of the board snapped tight. 'Hey, you're bleeding.'

'I got whacked, but not hard enough to do damage.' Or so she'd thought.

Strong fingers held her chin and tipped her head back gently. 'You're the doctor, but I'm thinking you're needing a couple of stitches on your chin.'

She began to feel a sharpness on the corner of her chin. 'Guess I'm going into work after all.' She didn't doubt he was right. He knew his medicine.

'I can take you to the weekend emergency surgery.

Though that will take longer, since you're not staff.'
Cody put his hands under her arms and hauled her up
to sprawl across his board. As easy as that. 'Stay still
and I'll paddle us back in.'

She shook her head. Was nothing too much trouble
for Cody Brand? He'd never used a board before yet he
was already turning them towards shore and calmly
pushing his paddle through the water despite that current. It would be too easy to get used to this, to come to
rely on him to look out for her.

Harper stiffened. No way. She watched her own back.
No one else did. Not even for a few weeks while they
had an affair. *Huh?* They were having an affair now?
Why not?

'You okay? You've gone quiet, and I don't like a quiet
Harper as much as the chatty one.' Above her, Cody was
smiling that heart-melting, 'I will take care of everything' smile that was his trademark.

'I'm thinking I like the sound of going to the surgery, wait or no wait.' There was less chance of people
from work knowing she and Cody had been spending
the day together.

'No problem. That cut hurting yet?'

'I'm trying to pretend it doesn't.' The sharp ache was
amplified with salt water sluicing over it as they bobbed
up and down. The daily summer sea breeze had arrived,
chopping the surface and adding to the pressure pushing them in a direction in which they didn't want to go.

But Cody had everything under control and within
a very short time he jumped off to push the board with
her still sprawled over it onto the beach. 'Here we go.'
He leaned down and lifted her up, placing her carefully
on her feet. 'Let me get that cord off your ankle.' He

looked across the beach to the van that the board-hire company operated from and waved. 'Give us a hand, will you, buddy?'

'Her sewing skills weren't too bad.' Cody dropped an arm lightly over Harper's shoulders as he led her out of the emergency surgery to a taxi he'd ordered.

She looked a little pale and those black threads weren't helping her appearance as she muttered, 'Two stitches, and the poor woman was terrified of making a mistake with you hovering over her. You're not a frustrated plastic surgeon, by any chance?'

'Me? Never. More into dress making,' he quipped.

'You have absolutely no problem laughing at yourself, do you?' There was wonder in her voice and those tired eyes.

'Don't see any problem with that. I know who I am and I'm totally comfortable with people having a laugh at me. Believe me, I'd never have survived nine years on the trawlers if I couldn't take the crap the guys threw at me. You're fair game with some of those rogues if you get too serious about just about anything.'

He felt her shudder under his arm. 'I've had a very sheltered life.'

'Huh? You can say that after our drug-runner incident? Or having dealt with Friday and Saturday night revellers and their drunken angst in the ED?'

'I guess.'

There'd been something else in her earlier comment. 'A previous partner didn't take kindly to being teased about his skills, or lack of?' Her history concerning partners was a complete mystery, and likely to stay that way, he acknowledged to himself.

But Harper did what she'd done last Sunday on the

beach. She blurted the truth quickly and emotionlessly. 'My husband had a great sense of humour except when it came to anything about himself.'

Husband? *Jeez.* Cody shoved his free hand through his hair. He did not do having sexual relations, sexual anything, with a married woman. 'I didn't know.'

'That I was married? I don't tend to make a big deal of it. It's an episode of my life I do not want to revisit.' She looked up at him and now there was emotion lining her voice. 'No point. What's done is finished.'

Phew. Was *married, not* is *married.* He could breathe easily again. 'How long have you been separated?' He should quit while he was ahead, but he liked learning little snippets of information about her. Marriage wasn't small, whether she'd separated or not. Okay, so he was nosey, or out to protect himself. He couldn't decide which.

'The divorce came through two months ago, right on the two-year anniversary of when we officially called it quits. I was in a hurry. If I wasn't going to be married in the full sense of the word then I wanted out.'

'I get that.' *I think.* But then he'd never been there; he would never have the chance to see his marriage through or leave it. That had been taken out of his hands by the man who'd killed Sadie.

'You ever been married? Or in a serious relationship?' Harper asked.

Don't want to go there. He could change the subject. But then he'd asked first. Which only went to show how much he lost the plot when he was around Harper. 'Yes. Years back. It lasted six months and then she died.'

'Cody.' Harper spun around to stand in front of him, her hands resting on his cheeks. 'I'm so sorry.'

His gut twisted at the sight of that genuine concern

for him. Her hands were soft and gentle on his cheeks. He placed a hand over one of hers and lifted it to kiss her palm. 'Me too.' Another kiss, then he stepped back.

'Don't want to talk about it?' There was no reproach in her eyes or her tone. Just a genuine concern that if he didn't want to carry on this conversation she'd be okay with that.

'Not really. It would spoil the day.' Wrapping his hand around her soft small one, he swung them high. 'I don't want to do that.'

'Then take me back to my place so I can change into something half-decent and we'll go out for a drink and dinner. My shout.'

'Yes to all of the above, except I'm shouting you.' When she began to argue he covered her mouth with his and kissed her, long and slowly, long enough for her hopefully to forget whatever she'd been going to say.

CHAPTER EIGHT

'WILL YOU LOOK at that?' Tim, one of the doctors clocking off from night shift, whistled as Harper took the notes he was handing her about a patient in Resus. 'Things get a little rough between you two over the weekend, did they?' He glanced from Harper to someone behind her.

Turning slightly, Harper saw Cody strolling in, looking totally ready for the start of the week and not at all as if he'd spent most of the weekend making love with her or doing other energetic activities.

Then, 'What did you say?' Cody snapped, that nonchalance gone in a flash.

'Joking, mate. Harper's chin looks like it's taken a nudge. What happened?' His question was directed at her.

But she didn't get a chance to answer.

Cody stepped up to Tim and growled, 'Nothing like what you're thinking.'

'Take it easy.' Tim stepped back. 'I said I was joking.'

'It's not a joke to suggest someone has been rough with a woman.'

Harper grabbed Cody's arm and pulled until he settled back down on the heels of his shoes. She shouldn't be touching him at work, but she had to get him to see sense. Quickly. 'Tim didn't mean anything. He certainly wasn't suggesting for one moment that you knocked me around.' Dropping her hand, she handed Cody a file. 'This patient's ours. Go and get her. Now.' She was talking to him as though he was a recalcitrant child, but he needed to get away from Tim and calm down.

'Yes, doctor,' Cody snapped, a flicker of hurt crossing his face before he all but snatched the file from her fingers. Tossing a glare at Tim, he turned to head for the waiting room.

Watching him stride away, his back über-straight, his head high, she said, 'I was paddle-boarding and fell off—took a hit on the chin.' What was bugging Cody, for him to go septic so fast? Had someone accused him of hitting a woman in the past? Surely not? He absolutely wouldn't do anything remotely violent—he was the proverbial gentle giant, except when confronted with a gunman in Resus. She'd swear her career on that, but that didn't mean someone hadn't accused him of some such action to get attention or make his life uncomfortable.

'Ambulance bringing in hit-and-run victim, male, twenty-four, cyclist. ETA fifteen—though it's the start of the rush hour, so that might go out further.' Karin had taken the call when Cody had headed for the waiting room on Harper's instructions.

'What's the damage?' Harper asked. Cyclists copped more than their share of shoulder injuries.

'Probable fractured clavicle, fractured humerus—otherwise nothing obvious,' Karin replied, unknowingly acknowledging Harper's thoughts.

'One for the orthopaedic crowd, then. You want to take him?'

Karin nodded. 'Absolutely. Thanks.'

'I'll be within calling distance.' She'd also look in on the situation regularly. Karin was a very competent registrar but it never hurt to make sure she didn't have any problems with a patient. Now, where had Cody got to?

There he was, escorting an elderly man and woman into Cubicle Two. His face was strained, though he spared a smile when the couple said something to him. 'Deep cut to thigh,' he told Harper in a less-than-friendly tone as she approached. 'Mr Gregory fell over the gardening fork and landed on some corrugated iron an hour ago.'

'He shouldn't have been digging the garden at all,' the woman Harper presumed was Mr Gregory's wife growled. 'He's been told to leave it to our boys.'

As Cody eased the man onto the bed, Mr Gregory retorted, 'I want to pick my veggies this summer, not next year. They never have time for a cup of tea, let alone to turn over the garden.'

'Maybe that's because you told them off last time they came to help.'

Okay, that was enough. Monday morning and crotchety patients—and nurses—was not how she wanted her week to start. 'Right, Mr Gregory. I'm Dr White. Nurse Brand says you've got a deep cut which we will probably have to sew back together. Let's take a look.'

While Cody removed the man's trousers, Harper turned to the woman. 'Mrs Gregory?' She nodded and Harper continued. 'Would you mind sitting over there? Thank you.' Right, everyone was in their place and she could get on with her day. Except she glanced at Cody and her heart softened. Whatever that altercation had been about, it had shaken him. There was a white line around his mouth, and his eyes were sending out spears to anyone who dared look at him, which was mostly her at the moment. *Well, I didn't do anything wrong.*

Cody looked up, those eyes wintry. 'I'll get the gear.' He nodded at the wound he'd exposed on the old man's thigh.

'Thanks.' She snapped on gloves and began to gently probe at the wound. 'When you do something you do it well, don't you, Mr Gregory? We're going to have a load of stitches in here by the time you go home.'

He winced when she touched the wound again. 'Yes, lass, I believe in doing a proper job, no matter what it is.'

'I bet you grow fabulous vegetables.' She chattered on to keep him occupied and hopefully not noticing too much pain. It also kept her mind off Cody and whatever his problem was.

'Do you grow a garden, doctor?'

'Can't say I've ever tried.' Could that be her next attempt to find something to do outside of work? No. She'd decided to give that up and focus on what she already had, hadn't she?

'Dr White is more attuned to sewing than digging.' That deep, husky voice came from behind her. The edgy tone had lightened a little.

It seemed she might almost be back in favour, though why she'd actually slipped out of it because of something Tim had said, she had yet to find out. 'And colour co-ordinating,' she risked. Looking directly at Cody, she was rewarded with a small smile, and knew everything was right between them again. Until she took him to task about his earlier reaction. That had not been good and, if the staff hadn't been aware they'd seen each other over the weekend, they certainly would be now.

'Mr Gregory.' Cody glanced at the older man. 'What

colour would you use for your bedroom if you were painting it?'

'Aw shucks, lad, ask the missus. She says I'm hopeless at that stuff, though I don't see anything wrong with a bit of strong colour myself.'

That set Mrs Gregory off on another tirade.

Harper hastened to finish suturing the wound, then left Cody to put a gauze cover over it while she went to print out a prescription for antibiotics and a mild analgesic for her patient.

'That chin looks sore,' Karin said. 'You must've hit the board hard.'

'It was the paddle that got me.' She signed the prescription. 'How was your weekend?'

'Quiet. Studied a lot, saw my sister for a bit, caught up on washing. Nothing exciting. No paddle-boarding with a hunk, for sure.'

Harper's teeth snapped tight. Then she forced herself to relax. This was no different from any other Monday morning except that she'd been with Cody over the weekend and didn't want everyone gossiping about them. 'I don't think I'll be doing it again.'

'What? Paddle-boarding or spending time with Hottie?'

Harper's brow tightened and she opened her mouth with a retort, only to be talked over by Karin.

'You shouldn't have left the pub looking like you were totally lost in each other if you didn't want people to know you'd get together.' The annoying woman nodded at her with a warning in her eyes. 'Stop letting everyone get to you and they'll soon find something or someone else to talk about.'

'But I haven't said anything.'

'Only yelled at Tim, stuck up for Cody and ignored

Jess when she asked you about your weekend.' Karin laughed lightly. 'So not like our well-mannered, polite and fun consultant at all.'

Harper pushed up from the chair. 'Thanks for the warning. I guess I did get a bit carried away.' But she'd been rocked by Cody's outburst. Would he tell her what it had been about? If they saw each other this week out of work, that was. 'Are you free to do dinner and a movie one night this week?'

'I am. Are you?' Karin winked and headed for the resus room.

I have no idea, Harper wondered as she headed back to Mr Gregory. *Yes, I will be. I can't cut off other friends because of one particular man.* She slipped into the cubicle and the breath caught in her throat at the sight of that man gently helping their patient back into his trousers while keeping the old man's dignity in place. 'Where have you been all my life, Cody Brand?'

'On a fishing trawler, getting on with *my* life,' he drawled as they watched the elderly couple walk towards the exit, Mrs Gregory giving her husband an earful about being more careful in the future.

Harper would've felt sorry for the old man if she hadn't noticed Mrs Gregory slip her hand into her husband's for a brief moment. Then she really heard Cody and her head shot up. 'Did I say that out loud?'

He nodded. 'You did. I'd ask what you meant by it but there's a waiting room full of patients, and a load of staff around here with ears bigger than their backsides.' He leaned over the counter for the patient files. 'Now, who's next?'

'My ears aren't that big.' Jess nudged him as she strolled past.

Harper took the file from Cody. 'I'll get this one.

You two continue your discussion on ears and butts.' She was back to normal, feeling relaxed and happy to be at work. The weekend had been one out of the box; it might or might not be repeated, minus the chin whack, and right now she was ready for anything.

As if to prove a point, the emergency phone screeched as she walked past. Though it was Cody's job to answer it, she automatically picked up the receiver. 'Wellington ED. Dr White.'

'Rescue helicopter service, doctor. Bee attack in the Sounds. Patient male, sixty-five, no known prior allergies. ETA twenty-five.' The woman called out more details.

'We'll be ready.' Harper put the phone down. 'We've got a severe allergic reaction coming in.'

Cody knew he'd overreacted to Tim's comment, but hey. He hated when someone went off half-cocked and didn't bother to find out the real deal. That caused people distress or at the very least unhappiness. It had happened with his mate, Jack: because of false accusations by his girlfriend about hitting her, he'd nearly ended up in jail.

Cody's gut churned. Harper had been unhappy with his reaction, and he couldn't blame her. There'd been searching looks from her all morning that shamed him. He should've shrugged Tim's comments away, as Harper had.

Come lunchtime, he went for a walk in the blazing sun and fierce wind to get some air to clear his head. He was an idiot not to explain to Harper why he'd reacted like that. It wasn't that big a deal, but he'd got used to keeping quiet about what mattered most to him after Sadie's passing. Was now the time to start opening up, start letting Harper in a little?

Harper. She was getting to him. Sneaking under his skin, rattling his beliefs and worrying him stupid.

After just one weekend he was ready to spend more time with her. He'd even consider—no, he'd go with—having an affair for as long as it lasted. But that was as far as he'd go. His heart would cope with that, but no more.

So why did he feel as though he'd known her for ever? Why did the idea that they had a future together keep blindsiding him? Why the feelings of wanting to protect her, to be there for her all the time, to share everything with her? He enjoyed being with her; he wanted more and couldn't wait to get into bed with her again. All this after such a short time.

'You going to stand there all day looking like someone stole your coffee?' Harper reached past him to drop a completed patient file on the desk.

'Sorry. Having a rest on my feet.' He looked around the department and saw nothing untoward. 'Who's next?'

'A toddler with a dislocated thumb. You want to go and get him?'

'Sure.' He loved his job. Even on days like today. Yet right now it would be great to be able to head away and take his confusion out with a hammer as he put the boards back on the railing of his veranda. Or to slop some paint on a couple of walls. Except he had yet to decide on the colour and buy the paint. Harper's suggestion of deep cream didn't quite turn him on. Like he knew anything about it. Cream could be anything; what did it matter about the shade he painted the place when he couldn't tell what it was?

Except he was determined to make his house something special, to do it up and decorate it in the style it had been built in ninety-odd years ago.

He returned to Harper. 'Want dinner at my place tonight? I'd like to run some decorating ideas past you.'

Surprise filled her eyes, and the smile she found for him was a little lopsided as she nodded slowly. 'I'd like that.'

'Six o'clock suit you? I need to visit the supermarket and do a couple of jobs before you get there.'

Her smile widened and tied his gut in more knots than usual while giving his heart a nudge. The fireworks between them were unbelievably intense, like something he'd never experienced. Or had forgotten over the last few years.

He wanted more of Harper. Hadn't even begun to have enough of her. It could be that he'd never have enough. Damn it.

The day was a continuous stream of patients. Harper began to wonder if three o'clock would ever arrive, but finally it did. 'I'm exhausted. That's got to have been the busiest day in a long while.'

'You said that one day last week.' Cody had joined her in the staff room.

'Really? I must need a break. It would be cool to go lie on a beach somewhere for a few days.' A beach, sun, water: it sounded wonderful. Sunburn, paddle-boards knocking her head, mosquitos... It still didn't sound half-bad if she compared it to drug overdoses, broken bones and cut hands. She checked her phone for messages; she'd got the usual texts from the brats, and one from her sister reminding her about Levi's birthday. 'As if I'd forget that.' She had a present to pick up. She might as well go to town now and then it was done, box ticked.

'Forget what?' Cody asked as his locker banged shut.

'Levi's birthday. I'm going shopping.' Then she remembered Cody had been invited to the party. 'Will you be joining us on the day?'

His hesitation made her hold her breath until he finally asked, 'Would you like me to?'

'Yes.' Definitely. 'Can't think of any reason why not.'

'Except for your family giving us a hard time, but I guess we can handle them.' He could have sounded like he wanted that, not uncertain and wary.

'Glad you think so. They've been soft on you so far.'

'Really? Can hardly wait for the next instalment.' He nodded. 'You want help picking a present? Before I go to the supermarket?'

'I've already ordered it. He wanted a wicket-keeper's glove.'

'Any suggestions on what I can get him?' Cody looked hopeful.

She spoilt that straight away. 'Nope. You'll have to come up with something yourself. So, let's take my car and I'll drop you back here later.'

'Sounds good.'

Hopefully some time that afternoon or tonight they'd get to talk about what had caused his abrupt mood change that morning. Because she really wanted to know. From his swift reaction to Tim, it was obviously something ingrained in him, what made him the man he was, and she needed to know more about this man who'd caught her when she wasn't looking. So much so that she wondered if she might've fallen a little bit in love.

A little bit? Or a massive, heart-stopping lot? *He wants a family, remember?* She wasn't likely to forget. But it seemed that hadn't stopped her heart getting involved here. Which could become a problem.

'I'll come if you promise not to nag me about anything.' His words were light but his eyes told her he was serious.

'We're not going to talk about what happened with Tim, then?'

'No. We're not.'

That stung. It seemed personal stuff was taboo. She'd gleaned a few bits of information here and there, but nothing deep and revealing. Was she prepared to talk about Darren and his change of heart over her inability to have children? Possibly. But then it was early on in their—their what? It wasn't a relationship. Not yet. Probably never would be. A fling? As in, meet for sex and fun when there was nothing else going on in their lives? Or something more, that involved sharing meals and movies and her family parties? 'Whatever.' She shrugged, knowing she must sound like a petulant teen. There were a few of those around the place today.

Walking out to her car, they were both quiet. Harper was trying to move past her disappointment. She had no right to expect Cody to talk about private issues when she wasn't prepared to be totally open with him. That didn't mean she didn't want to push the buttons that would make him tell all.

'You're over-thinking everything.'

She pinged the locks on her car but instead of sitting inside in the heat that had built up over the day she leaned against the door, her arms folded on the roof, her chin on her wrist, and eyeballed Cody. 'I do that when I haven't got any clues to work with.'

He mimicked her stance from the other side, his gaze firmly on her, as though he was weighing up what to say. 'I'm sorry for the way I reacted this morning. It was a hangover from the past.'

Harper waited. That wasn't enough of an explanation.

His sigh was loud between them as he gave in. 'My close mate's girlfriend got drunk and fell off a balcony into a garden, collecting some massive bruises on the way. She used it against Jack, saying he hit her. Fortunately, her timing was out. We were still on board the trawler tied up at the wharf at the time. As it was, no one believed Jack until someone came forward to say they'd seen the woman fall.'

'That stinks.' How could anyone do that?

'It screwed Jack's life. Some people couldn't accept the truth and kept pointing the finger. He finally moved across the Tasman to settle in Perth.'

So he'd lost a close friend out of it all as well. 'I think I can understand your comments to Tim now.'

'But I should be toning them down? I get it. Sometimes I forget I'm not working amongst fishermen any more. He probably didn't mean anything by it.' He finally smiled. A tight, sad smile, but a smile.

Of course, that got him exactly what he wanted. 'Get in.'

As she drove towards the sports shop where she'd ordered Levi's present, her brain was busy thinking over the little that Cody had said. 'What made you decide to become a nurse?'

'Thought you were being too quiet,' Cody muttered. At least he was still smiling. 'You don't give up easily, do you?'

'I don't see what's wrong with asking that.'

His sigh hissed over his lips. 'Nothing, I guess.' He stretched his legs as far as possible, not far at all, considering how long they were. 'Okay, no. I always wanted to be a nurse right from when I was at school.' He stopped.

As she accelerated away from traffic lights, she asked, 'So?'

'I was a rebel, having too much fun with outdoor stuff to settle into more study. I was also intent on proving that the snide remarks suggesting I was a girl if I was going to be a nurse were wrong. What testosterone-laden teen isn't going to react by proving how masculine he is?' He grinned at her.

Harper chuckled. 'There's nothing girlie about you.' She knew intimately. Whipping into a vacant parking space right outside her destination, she stopped the engine. How lucky was that? 'Did you ever consider becoming a doctor?'

'Briefly, but nursing always held more interest for me. Anyway, by the time I was ready to change careers, I'd spent too long doing a very physical job. The extra years and the huge hours studying for a medical degree would've stifled me.'

'That makes sense.' Then, 'What happened to make you leaving fishing and go after your original dream?'

'Let's quit the questions, shall we?' There was a hint of anger in his voice. His door opened and he swung his legs out.

'I'm interested, that's all.' What was going on? The man was moody as all hell today. It didn't seem to matter what she said, she got it wrong.

He glared at her over his shoulder. 'Harper, drop it. I don't need this.' He stood up and closed the door with a little shove.

When she clambered out, she said, 'Sorry. But it was a simple question, nothing more. All part of getting to know you better.'

'You don't know when to quit, do you?' He blanched. Stepped back. Shook his head at her. 'We'll take a rain check on that dinner.' Then he walked away, leaving her wondering what had just happened.

She watched him charge through the crowds of shoppers and office workers, heading back the way they'd come, his shoulders tight, his head forward. *Did I really deserve that?*

Maybe. He disliked talking about himself, yet she'd kept pushing. But she wanted to know Cody, as in everything about him. They were getting close, had spent that amazing weekend together; of course she wanted to understand what made him tick, why he reacted to situations like he did.

So how dared he speak to her like that? She *didn't* deserve it; didn't need him to bite her head off.

He'd said 'a rain check' for dinner. Did he think she'd be hanging around waiting eagerly for his next invitation? He could go take a flying leap. She didn't do that for anyone.

CHAPTER NINE

HARPER PARKED AT work and shoved the door open, then grabbed it as a gust of wind blew through the car park. 'Whoa.' The image in her mind of her door bent back on its hinges was not pretty.

Not that there was a lot that looked good in there this morning. Cody had dominated her thoughts throughout the long night, and was still there now.

Her head throbbed with discontentment.

One weekend with Cody had not been enough. But she'd probably walk into the department and he'd be there with his smile, acting as though he hadn't walked away from her yesterday. *You wish.* Was he a man who forgave easily? But then, what was there to forgive? She'd done, said, nothing out of the ordinary as far as she could see.

During those long hours of the night, she'd begun wondering why he'd reacted so angrily, so quickly, to what she'd asked. Every answer she came up with had no substance—because she didn't know him well enough.

Out of the car, the wind caught at her hair, pulling strands loose from the band she'd wound round it earlier. Typical Wellington day—or so the rest of the country thought.

The roar of a motorbike told her that Cody had arrived. Should she wait for him and risk being snubbed? Or should she head inside and pull on her scrubs in readiness for another day?

Unwilling to be snubbed, she took the soft option. They had all day for her find out where she stood with him.

'Hey, Harper,' Cody said as she made her way to shift change-over.

'Morning,' she acknowledged, watching him walk to the changing room and wondering if that had been a friendly or not-so-friendly tone he'd used. Then thought, *this is plain childish. Of me and him.* She didn't do childish. She often growled at the brats for that. Thank goodness they weren't here to witness her slide from the rules. Right, she'd act as though yesterday hadn't happened when Cody joined the group.

She didn't get a chance to act in any way at all. An ambulance brought in two men from a truck that had gone over the edge of a bridge spanning the motorway. A serious spinal injury took all Harper's concentration for the next hour and a half.

Cody worked alongside her, friendly enough, but still with a glimmer of reproach in his attitude.

And that was how the week continued. The ease they'd known the previous week had gone, leaving them back to being two members of the day shift who got along fine as long as they stuck to work issues.

'You need some sleep,' Karin told her on Friday as they were winding up and handing over to the night shift. 'Hope you've got a quiet weekend ahead.'

'A birthday party with the brat pack.' Yikes, was Cody still going to join her family for that?

Apparently so. Sunday afternoon at Jason's again,

and Cody was playing cricket. Again. Harper was having a wine with her sister and sisters-in-law. Again.

She couldn't believe Cody had turned up after the
week they'd had keeping their distance with each other.
It didn't make any sense. As soon as the game stopped,
she was going to bail him in a corner and demand to
know what he thought he was doing.

Jason handed her a refilled glass. 'What's the lover's
tiff about, then?'

'You want to wear this?' Harper held her glass up.

'That'd be a waste.'

'Then go play with the kids.'

Surprisingly, he did, and Harper started to relax a
little.

Until Suzanne picked up where their brother had left
off. 'Want to talk about it?'

Silly girl. She should've known better with her family. 'No.'

'So something's happened.'

The wine was chilled to perfection, but suddenly
she wasn't enjoying it. 'Why does everyone think because Cody and I aren't falling all over each other there's
something wrong? We work together, we're not soul
mates.'

Gemma looked from her across to where Cody was
bowling the ball and back again. 'Could've fooled me.
You've both had the hots for each other right from that
day the gunman held his weapon to your head. The way
Cody carried you up the path to your apartment was so
tender and loving, it made me all gooey inside.'

Harper could recall in a flash every detail, every
sensation of those strong arms holding her against that
wide chest. Now she knew his body better, she wanted

more. Lots more. '"Loving" is a big word. We'd hardly talked until that day.'

'If it fits,' Gemma quipped. 'You two sure look like it does.'

'What's really the problem?' Suzanne asked.

Everything. Nothing. She wasn't telling them the nitty gritty of their argument when she hadn't figured it out herself, but she could raise what would eventually become the final devastating issue between her and Cody. 'He wants kids.'

'You've discussed this?'

'He told me the weekend we rode out to Pencarrow Head.' How could she have been so stupid as to think she could manage this? Could walk away from the best thing she'd ever known? Cody was...the man she'd fallen for. In a flash. Probably from the first time she'd taken notice of his hot bod in scrubs. He was everything she wanted in a man and a whole heap more.

Talk about setting herself up to get hurt. She couldn't blame anyone else. She also couldn't continue with the relationship—if it was still there.

'Writing this relationship off before you have a full and frank discussion with Cody is a bit like cutting your own throat when you're actually happy.'

Sisters could be so annoying and interfering. 'You think after Darren I'm going to put my heart on the line when I already know Cody has desires for a family of his own?'

'There are other options. Adoption. Surrogate mothers. It goes on all the time.'

'Why would Cody do that when he doesn't have to?'

'Because he loves you.'

Harper leapt to her feet, the wine flying through the air. 'Don't say that!' she yelled at Suzanne. *I can't cope with that.* 'What would you know? Next you'll be saying I love him.'

'Don't you?'

Yeah, she did. She'd finally admitted it to herself. But for her family to see it, that made it harder to pretend otherwise. 'Shut up.'

'There a problem here?' Cody had strolled across the lawn to stand a couple of metres away. He might have thought his expression was neutral but Harper would have sworn she could detect hurt lurking in his eyes and in the slight downturn of his mouth.

He'd overheard Suzanne. Or her. More likely her. She'd been the one yelling. 'Yes. Annoying sisters who don't know when to mind their own business.'

'Time for a bike ride, out where we went the other day.' Cody held out his hand. 'You need a jacket.'

'Excuse me?' She stared at him. Dropped her gaze to that extended hand. Extended in friendship? What else? But go with him on a ride so that he could quiz her about what he thought he'd overheard?

'Harper?' Cody asked. 'Jacket.'

So he wasn't taking no for an answer. Not that she'd given any response. She felt incapable of one. Had no damned idea what she should be doing. Going back to where they'd had their first kiss hummed with danger.

Behind her there was utter silence.

The easy option would be to go with him. At least as far as the gate. She had to get away from the girls. Needed time to think without their crazy input.

Harper grimaced as Cody revved the bike and headed for the main road. How much of that argument with her sisters had he heard? She cringed when she thought he might've overheard the 'love' word.

For the first time holding on to him was a nightmare.

Putting her arms around him made her want to cry for what they might've had. For that love she held for him but couldn't share. On an indrawn breath, she laid her face against his back. She felt his strength wherever she touched him; the strength that had drawn her to him in the first place.

It was as though she had to feel him, to smell him, be with him for one last day to store memories to take out in the middle of the night over the coming weeks and months.

The ride was torture. Time was running out. After today, they'd definitely be over. She would call it off. Falling in love with Cody had wrecked the hopeful fallacy that she could have fun with him without getting hurt.

At Pencarrow Cody helped Harper off the bike and walked beside her along the beach. He said nothing, but his head was spinning, his gut churning. She hadn't denied she loved him when Suzanne had pressed her. Gees. He jammed his fingers through his hair. Jeez. What was he supposed to do with that little gem of information?

Even as he wanted to lift her into his arms and spin them round in circles while grinning and kissing her, he fought not to run for his bike and take off as fast as it could go in an attempt to outrun the fear driving up through him. He couldn't do this, whatever 'this' was. He wanted to love Harper back, to have the whole family, home and Sundays playing cricket thing. He really, really did. But what if he lost Harper like he'd lost Sadie? What if someone like that lowlife with his gun happened again? What if...? A hundred questions exploded through his brain, none of them stopping for an answer.

They reached the end of the beach, both pausing to stare around as though they had no idea why they were there. *Well, hello, I don't. I dragged Harper here and now I don't know what to do, what to say.*

He certainly wasn't about to tell her he was frightened of what might be blooming between them. If it still was after the last hour.

Finally he asked, 'Why did your marriage break up?' *Why that question?* He'd no idea, but it seemed a good place to start.

'Darren left me because I couldn't have babies.' Her voice was quiet but determined. As though she wanted this over.

'You hadn't told him before you married?'

Now her voice rose and anger spat at him. 'Thanks a bunch. You honestly think that I'd hide something so important from the man I loved?' She dropped to sit on the damp sand. 'You believe I kept quiet in the hope he'd accept it once we were married?'

'That's not what I said. Not quite,' he admitted with a hint of guilt. 'I know you better than that.'

'I thought you did.' She shook her head. 'But really, I know very little about you, and the same could be said the other way round.'

He stared down at her, his heart beating hard and loud. 'So Darren just changed his mind?'

'Yes. After we'd been married for two years. After all his promises about finding other means to have our own family.'

Cody squatted down beside her. He wanted to take her hands in his, but even as he began to reach for her his old fear prevailed. Why touch her when he didn't want to continue a relationship with her? *As in, a marriage and happy-ever-after relationship? Who said you don't want it?* He did want it, badly, but he couldn't do it. Today, after hearing what she'd said to Suzanne, he knew he couldn't. Knew that he'd always live with the fear of something bad happening to her, of him losing her one way or another.

He picked up a small stone and hurled it at the sea. 'You got a raw deal.'

'Huh? You reckon?' Leaping to her feet, she stormed down to the water's edge, her small hands clenched into fists at her sides.

He followed, stood beside her and waited impatiently. For what, he didn't know, but there was more to come. It was there in her stance, in her face. Did he want to hear it? Yeah, he did. For whatever reason, he did.

I love him. Harper gulped, drew in a deep breath and squeezed her eyes shut. She loved Cody. End of. Yes, very much the end of.

Her anger intensified. How stupid could she get? Loving Cody was impossible. Not allowed. She'd never ask him to give up his dream of a family for her. Never. She kicked at the water, got splashed for her effort.

'What went wrong for your husband to change his mind?' Cody stood so close to her she could feel his heat, yet the gap between them felt as wide as the Cook Strait.

'What's the point of all this?' she snapped.

'Then I'd know.' He sounded so damned reasonable.

'Right. Then will you tell me why you never talk about your past? I doubt it.' The air from her lungs hissed over her lips. 'Take me back. Now. I'm done with this, with you.' They had to break up one day, so it might as well be today when they were already at loggerheads.

Cody looked away, went back to staring at that blasted stretch of water between the two heads.

'I loved Sadie very much.'

Harper waited, her temper not abating, but hovering, ready to explode. She wanted to hear him out, but he had to hurry. Her patience was at zero. Because she was hurting.

'When I said she'd died…' He paused and slowly met her gaze. 'She was murdered.'

Slam. Her anger evaporated. Instantly she reached for his hand. It was cold in hers. 'Oh, Cody, that's appalling.'

'She divorced her ex when he went to prison for fraud. We met around that time and fell head over heels in love, got married as soon as she was free, and life was sweet. Or so we thought.'

Harper continued holding his hand, shocked at what she was hearing.

'I came home from work one day to find her lying in the lounge, bleeding out. I couldn't save her. She never stood a chance once he stabbed her heart.'

Cody's voice broke. 'He planned it so I'd find her. He wanted me to pay for marrying his wife. He'd learned when I was home from a fishing trip, escaped from jail, headed straight for our house and waited until he heard me turn into the drive.' Tears streamed down his cheeks. 'I tried to save her. I did everything possible. It wasn't enough.'

'If her heart was stabbed it's doubtful anyone could've done any better.'

'That's what the doctors told me. Didn't help at all.'

That was when he'd changed careers; she'd bet on it. Wrapping her arms around him, she held him tight, feeling the ripples of anguish shaking his body.

It was a long time before Cody stepped away. He didn't say anything.

Harper told him, 'I'm sorry I made you relive that.' She couldn't not tell him now that he'd shared his horrific story. She owed him that much. 'Darren said he didn't care about not being able to have children with me. But he changed his mind and got another woman pregnant before he left me. Kind of like insurance, making sure the next woman in his life was fertile.' The past was sour in her mouth. 'I should be over this by now. I guess I am in some ways, but I'll never trust another man about this again.'

More hurt spilled into Cody's eyes.

She was sorry for that, but the truth needed to be put between them. 'Don't take it personally. It's just I couldn't stand to have my heart broken again.'

'You think I can?'

'I understand you can't.'

'So where does that leave us?' he asked.

She swore under her breath. She loved him. But... 'Even knowing each other's history, understanding the pain we've both been through, caring about each other...' She *thought* he cared for her. 'What you and I have had isn't going anywhere. It can't. There's a fundamental flaw in us having a long-term relationship. You would like a family. I can't have one.' She had to remind him, to put it out there again, just so that he didn't try to avoid it. 'End of.'

'Thanks for nothing, Harper.'

'Cody.' she sighed. She could go on explaining herself, but what was the point? He'd understand more than most how she didn't want to be hurt again. But would he understand she didn't want to hurt *him*? 'Can you take me back to my family?'

* * *

Cody wanted to race the bike down the motorway, break every speed restriction there was, go so fast he couldn't think.

But he didn't. Common sense prevailed. Just.

So Harper went home with him—in his head. Her words sliced him to shreds. They were finished. On her terms. *End of.*

'End of what, Harper?' he yelled as he flung the bike around the corner of his street. 'I go and fall in love with you and you say it's over.'

Not that he'd fessed up to his feelings. That old fear of getting hurt had raised its head the moment he'd opened his mouth to tell her he loved her back there on the beach. He'd wanted to, almost more than anything, but he hadn't been able to say the words.

This morning he'd left home excited to be seeing Harper, and determined to move past the chilly week they'd endured, to resume their affair and move forward. He'd also been looking forward to spending time with her family. They'd drawn him in, made him comfortable and relaxed, eager to share their lives.

But at Jason's place he'd heard the girls arguing, overheard Harper's sister saying she loved him and Harper not denying it. That had caused something deep inside his heart to crack wide open. Love had spilled out, blinding him into thinking it might be possible to banish his fears. Then she'd dropped her bomb. She wasn't having a relationship with him.

Which just went to prove he'd been right to remain uninvolved in the first place. Except he hadn't; he had got in so deep there was no way out.

He loved Harper. No ifs, buts or maybes. He loved her. And she'd tossed him. Easy as.

No. Be fair. Not so, if that anger and pain in her eyes was anything to go by. There'd be no going back on her statement, though. Her chin had jutted out in a 'don't argue' gesture. Her hands had become fists at his waist as they'd ridden back to her brother's house. And her abrupt nod goodbye had been like a knife to his heart.

At home he tore his helmet off and banged it down on the outdoor table by the garage.

Now what? He could open a load of beers and get blind drunk, or he could start on getting that railing fixed. Or he could grab one beer and sort the railing. *Good idea.*

He could also try and figure out where to from here with Harper. *Hell.* He slammed his fingers through his hair. He hadn't got over the shock of realising he loved her yet. Loved her so much he'd go to the end of the earth for her.

No, he wouldn't; he couldn't. That was terrifying. Pain had wedged in his heart today but it'd only get worse if he tried to follow through on his feelings. Harper had made his mind up for him about having children; she wasn't letting him decide if he wanted them more than her. Why did she of all people do that? He'd been making his own mind up about everything he did from the day he'd learned to talk, yet she'd just walked all over him.

Which might be why Harper had got under his skin and annoyed the hell out of him. She wasn't even giving him a chance to work out what he wanted, what was best for them both. She'd made a decision and that was that. He was not used to it.

From the day he'd walked out of those school gates he'd worked damned hard, had become wealthy by using his hands and brain and could hold his head high.

Cody drained the beer bottle in his hand and stared up at the building in front of him, waiting for the usual pride to suffuse his chest. This house stood as a testament to his success.

Though it might turn out to be a lonely dwelling if he couldn't have Harper with him. His heart was now hers. What he did about that was still up in the air. Telling her he loved her and asking her to share his life meant exposing his fears. Not tell her, and he'd be giving up his dreams of a loving woman and family at his side. Harper was that woman. As for the children, they'd work something out if they were serious about each other.

Yep, which was why he'd start on nailing up that railing. He always thought best when doing manual work. Hopefully by the end of the day he'd have some answers.

The next week crept past so slowly, Harper thought she must've slept through a weekend and worked two weeks in a row.

On Friday afternoon she handed over to the incoming shift and slunk away quietly, not looking in Cody's direction once. She couldn't bear to see that sad expression that had been in his eyes every day since Sunday. He'd managed to avoid working with her most of the time, and in the few cases they'd shared he'd been exemplary in his manner towards her.

She hit the supermarket, trying to dredge up enthusiasm for something to cook for dinner. Nothing appealed. Not even ice-cream or chocolate. Ironic, when the week before she'd been pretending to diet, and this week she was struggling to put anything in her mouth.

The meat chillers held nothing to interest her. The deli came up short too. Talk about being picky. Harper crossed to the fish cabinet. Last try before she went home to eat an apple.

'I do a mean baked salmon and salad.'

The shopping basket clattered to the floor as the voice that had been haunting her every night of the past week caught her attention. 'Cody.'

He picked up the basket and swung it between them. 'Do you like salmon?'

What if she did? They weren't sharing a meal, not when they'd barely shared a sentence all week. She tried for a shrug but didn't do so well. 'Sometimes.'

'Would tonight be one of those times? With a glass of Pinot Gris? On my veranda overlooking the harbour?' He didn't beg, but there was a lot of entreaty in the way he looked at her.

'Why?' She had to know if this was a 'let's make up and be friends' gesture, or something more intense and serious. Or had he come up with his own reasons why they couldn't be together?

'We need to talk. About a lot of things.' Lightly swinging the basket between them again, he locked those spring-green eyes on her. 'I've missed you.'

'You've seen me every day.' Her heart began to thump a little harder and faster than was normal.

'I've still missed you.'

Her next breath hitched in her throat. Damn the man. He had a way with words. Add in the longing in his eyes, and the softest smile now curving his lips upwards, and what could she say? How could she refuse him when she'd missed him every minute, every second, of the past week? She turned to the woman waiting on the other side of the cabinet. 'I'll take that whole salmon, thank you.'

Suddenly she was ravenous.

* * *

The small talk Cody and Harper managed for the next hour as they drove to his house and prepared dinner wasn't too bad. They discussed work and her family, and where Harper thought she might go for her summer break that she'd apparently put in for yesterday.

'Why Rarotonga?' he asked, genuinely puzzled. 'Now's the windy season, isn't it?'

'I want lots of beach and warm water, and no paddle-boards.'

'Your chin looks okay now that the stitches are gone.' The tiny scar on the edge of her jawline was cute, and had him wanting to run his fingertip over it. He refrained from that mad idea. That could be pushing the boundaries. Yet some time tonight he'd have to. There were too many unsaid things lying between them that had to be confronted before he and Harper could move forward—together. He was determined they were heading into the future together.

With the salmon cooking slowly on the barbecue and the salad made, all that needed doing was to blanch the asparagus at the last minute. 'Let's take our wine outside.'

Harper followed and took a chair opposite him, which kind of suggested she wasn't quite as comfortable yet as he'd hoped.

Leaning across the table, he topped up her glass, then his, sat back and said, 'When Sadie died so did I.' He saw when she got it.

Her mouth softened and her eyes widened. She reached across the table to slip her hand into his. 'Go on.'

That was it, really. His chest rose as he drew in air. *Get this over with.* 'I'm afraid of losing someone I love again. That's why I let you push me away with no argument when you said we couldn't have a relationship because of your infertility. I want to change that. To prove I am better than that. To share your life—for ever, if you'll let me.'

She jerked her hand away, her eyes widening as she fixed him with a glare. 'You're feeling sorry for me?'

His fingers shot through his hair. Would they ever be able to have a conversation without misinterpreting everything? 'No, Harper. I don't. Well, I do, but my actions aren't based on sympathy.' *What actions? You haven't done anything yet except dig an even bigger hole to climb into.* 'I love you.'

She gaped at him.

He hadn't planned to say that yet; he'd thought he'd work up to it. But now some of the tension gripping him had starting easing, so he said it again. 'I love you. I knew it from the moment Lowlife held that gun to your head, and when after the initial shock you showed you cared as much for your patient as anything else that was happening. You're one gutsy lady.'

After a couple of beats, she said, 'I *was* scared witless when that gun banged against my skull.'

'Still a...'

'Let me finish.' She rubbed her temples in the way she had when she'd been getting a migraine. 'I'm scared way beyond that now. I love you too, Cody. Love you with every cell of my body. And that makes me afraid too.'

He didn't relax even as the thrill of hearing those words rolled through him. There was more to come. He saw it in her eyes. And he wasn't going to like it.

'Because of that, I am walking away from you, from us. I can never ask you to give up your chance of having a family. I can't and I won't. It would be selfish of me.'

'There are other ways to have children.'

Her head moved back and forth, back and forth, as though warding off his words. 'I heard that last time, but in the end it didn't happen.'

And she couldn't deal with the heartbreak again. He got it. In spades. He didn't have the words to persuade her to rethink her stance, so he stood and went to her, pulled her into his arms and held her tight, close to him, so they absorbed each other's warmth and tenderness. His chin rested on her head and he closed his eyes, absorbing every little movement she made, every place where her body touched his.

She pressed hard against him, her cheek against his chest, her hands around his waist, her breast moving up and down softly as she breathed.

He inhaled her citrus scent. Remembered that first kiss they'd shared. The kiss that had changed everything for him, had had him wondering if he could take a chance with her. Had had him doing it again at work, of all places.

They stood that way for a long time. Then Cody leaned back in her arms until he could see her face, saw when tears began to streak down her cheeks. Bending forward, he began to kiss her, murmuring, 'Don't cry, my love,' against her mouth. 'We're in this together.'

She stilled just as she'd begun nibbling his lip. Her mouth left his, making him feel chilled until he saw the warmth in her eyes.

'No one's ever said that to me before,' she whispered.

'It's true. I can't leave you. I won't, unless you push me away. All I ask is that you accept me as I am.' He had to trust that she would.

'Yes, of course I do.'

'Harper, will you marry me? Live with me for ever,

or at least until I'm old and grey and can't get it up any more to pleasure you?'

Harper's eyes widened in astonishment and a small, nervous laugh escaped her. 'That is a long way off, I'm sure. I've seen how easily you react to me when we're getting up close.' Then she sobered. 'What about children?'

'Sweetheart, there are ways. You know there are.' But he named a couple anyway. 'Surrogacy, for one. Adoption, for another. Or fostering, if you prefer. Quite frankly, it's more important that I'm with you. I love you so much, it's unbearable to even contemplate not being with you for the rest of my life. Children or no children.'

'I haven't told you, but I'd like a family too.' Her voice was soft and filled with a deep longing that broke his heart.

'Now who's trying to surprise who? I've seen you with the brat pack. I know how loving you are with each and every one of them. We'll do our damnedest to add to the pack one way or another.'

'Then, yes, darling Cody. I can't think of anything I want more than to marry you.'

He lifted her into his arms and swung her around. His heart beat rapidly, filled with love for this amazing woman who'd battered down all his resistance with very little effort just by being herself. 'I love you so much it hurts at times.'

'Then I'd better kiss you better.' Harper's mouth covered his in what turned out to be the longest, hottest kiss they'd experienced to date, and was only the beginning of greater things.

EPILOGUE

HARPER HELD THE precious little bundle wrapped in a woollen blanket cautiously in her arms and leaned her head against Cody's hip. Unbelievable. To be holding their daughter was beyond her wildest dreams. 'Isn't she beautiful?' she whispered.

'Very,' he croaked.

She looked up to see tears streaming down his cheeks and dripping off his chin. This man was full of emotion today. He had been since the moment the phone had rung at four in the morning to say Gemma had gone into labour. She loved that he showed his feelings. 'I think she looks like her dad.'

'I don't have a red scrunched-up face.' He dashed his forearm over his face.

'What do you think, Keely Tricia Gemma Brand? Does your dad look like you?'

'That's such a mouthful. Can't we drop two of the names, just call her Keely Brand? Think of her having to write that list down every time she fills in a document.'

'Absolutely not. I like using your mother's name as her second one and, as for Gemma, well, what can I say?' Tears welled up in her eyes and dripped down her face. Gemma was a star in her book.

She'd never forget the day, a month after their fabulous wedding, when Gemma and Jason had rocked up at the house looking so serious she'd feared for bad news. But, no; they'd come to suggest that Gemma be a surrogate mother for them. They'd stunned both her and Cody into silence for a long time. The idea had seemed wonderful, impossible, crazy, filled with so many problems that they should've said no.

Neither of them had been able to. Months of tests, counselling and talking to their families had followed before Gemma had finally been able to become pregnant for Cody and Harper through artificial insemination. Finally, Harper was a mum and Cody was a dad. A very proud one, by the look of wonder on his face.

'Here, your turn to hold her.' Harper didn't want to let Keely go but she held their daughter up to him, and smiled when he stepped back.

'Hell, no. I'll break her, or drop her or something.'

'You've held babies at work. You're going to be fine with your daughter.' Harper pressed Keely into his arms, watching the wonder grow as he gazed down at his beautiful bundle.

'Hello, sweetheart. Welcome to our world. I promise I'm going to try to be the best damned father ever.'

He would be. Harper already knew he was the best damned husband. Ever.

* * * * *

MILLS & BOON®
Hardback – August 2016

ROMANCE

The Di Sione Secret Baby	Maya Blake
Carides's Forgotten Wife	Maisey Yates
The Playboy's Ruthless Pursuit	Miranda Lee
His Mistress for a Week	Melanie Milburne
Crowned for the Prince's Heir	Sharon Kendrick
In the Sheikh's Service	Susan Stephens
Marrying Her Royal Enemy	Jennifer Hayward
Claiming His Wedding Night	Louise Fuller
An Unlikely Bride for the Billionaire	Michelle Douglas
Falling for the Secret Millionaire	Kate Hardy
The Forbidden Prince	Alison Roberts
The Best Man's Guarded Heart	Katrina Cudmore
Seduced by the Sheikh Surgeon	Carol Marinelli
Challenging the Doctor Sheikh	Amalie Berlin
The Doctor She Always Dreamed Of	Wendy S. Marcus
The Nurse's Newborn Gift	Wendy S. Marcus
Tempting Nashville's Celebrity Doc	Amy Ruttan
Dr White's Baby Wish	Sue MacKay
For Baby's Sake	Janice Maynard
An Heir for the Billionaire	Kat Cantrell

MILLS & BOON®
Large Print – August 2016

ROMANCE

The Sicilian's Stolen Son — Lynne Graham
Seduced into Her Boss's Service — Cathy Williams
The Billionaire's Defiant Acquisition — Sharon Kendrick
One Night to Wedding Vows — Kim Lawrence
Engaged to Her Ravensdale Enemy — Melanie Milburne
A Diamond Deal with the Greek — Maya Blake
Inherited by Ferranti — Kate Hewitt
The Billionaire's Baby Swap — Rebecca Winters
The Wedding Planner's Big Day — Cara Colter
Holiday with the Best Man — Kate Hardy
Tempted by Her Tycoon Boss — Jennie Adams

HISTORICAL

The Widow and the Sheikh — Marguerite Kaye
Return of the Runaway — Sarah Mallory
Saved by Scandal's Heir — Janice Preston
Forbidden Nights with the Viscount — Julia Justiss
Bound by One Scandalous Night — Diane Gaston

MEDICAL

His Shock Valentine's Proposal — Amy Ruttan
Craving Her Ex-Army Doc — Amy Ruttan
The Man She Could Never Forget — Meredith Webber
The Nurse Who Stole His Heart — Alison Roberts
Her Holiday Miracle — Joanna Neil
Discovering Dr Riley — Annie Claydon

MILLS & BOON®
Hardback – September 2016

ROMANCE

To Blackmail a Di Sione	Rachael Thomas
A Ring for Vincenzo's Heir	Jennie Lucas
Demetriou Demands His Child	Kate Hewitt
Trapped by Vialli's Vows	Chantelle Shaw
The Sheikh's Baby Scandal	Carol Marinelli
Defying the Billionaire's Command	Michelle Conder
The Secret Beneath the Veil	Dani Collins
The Mistress That Tamed De Santis	Natalie Anderson
Stepping into the Prince's World	Marion Lennox
Unveiling the Bridesmaid	Jessica Gilmore
The CEO's Surprise Family	Teresa Carpenter
The Billionaire from Her Past	Leah Ashton
A Daddy for Her Daughter	Tina Beckett
Reunited with His Runaway Bride	Robin Gianna
Rescued by Dr Rafe	Annie Claydon
Saved by the Single Dad	Annie Claydon
Sizzling Nights with Dr Off-Limits	Janice Lynn
Seven Nights with Her Ex	Louisa Heaton
The Boss's Baby Arrangement	Catherine Mann
Billionaire Boss, M.D.	Olivia Gates

MILLS & BOON®
Large Print – September 2016

ROMANCE

Morelli's Mistress	Anne Mather
A Tycoon to Be Reckoned With	Julia James
Billionaire Without a Past	Carol Marinelli
The Shock Cassano Baby	Andie Brock
The Most Scandalous Ravensdale	Melanie Milburne
The Sheikh's Last Mistress	Rachael Thomas
Claiming the Royal Innocent	Jennifer Hayward
The Billionaire Who Saw Her Beauty	Rebecca Winters
In the Boss's Castle	Jessica Gilmore
One Week with the French Tycoon	Christy McKellen
Rafael's Contract Bride	Nina Milne

HISTORICAL

In Bed with the Duke	Annie Burrows
More Than a Lover	Ann Lethbridge
Playing the Duke's Mistress	Eliza Redgold
The Blacksmith's Wife	Elisabeth Hobbes
That Despicable Rogue	Virginia Heath

MEDICAL

The Socialite's Secret	Carol Marinelli
London's Most Eligible Doctor	Annie O'Neil
Saving Maddie's Baby	Marion Lennox
A Sheikh to Capture Her Heart	Meredith Webber
Breaking All Their Rules	Sue MacKay
One Life-Changing Night	Louisa Heaton